THE NIGHTMARE CHRONICLE

JAYARAJ MENON

Made with ♥ on the Notion Press Platform
www.notionpress.com

Contents

About the Author   *v*

Preface   *vii*

1. HAUNTED HIGH NOON: AYYAPPAN OR THE TRICKSTER SPIRIT OF KORAPPAN?   1

2. CRYPTIC SHADOWS: 'VENGARA KOTHA'   9

3. TRYST WITH THE LURKING SOULS OF ARAKKAL GRAVEYARD   14

4. TIPPU AND THE EXORCIST   18

5. 'POTTI' THE MISCHIEVOUS SPIRIT   23

6. THE EERIE CAVERNS OF NARIMALAN KUNNU   29

7. ETHEREAL ENIGMA: THE SORCERER AND FORSAKEN HUT   37

8. LONGING FOR SALVATION: THE TALE OF AN UNSATIATED SPIRIT   43

9. PILGRIMAGE TO SABARIMALA AND THE MYSTERIOUS MECHANIC   48

10. WHISPERS IN THE DARK: STORY OF A HAUNTED APARTMENT   55

11. SHADOWS OF ETERNITY: A NIGHT IN THIRUVATTUR   68

12. THE GHOST WHO CAME TO WATCH TELEVISION   82

13. BRUSH WITH DANGER: SLITHERY SCARE IN THE NIGHT   88

14. CHILLS IN THE NIGHT: A GHOST IN THE TOILET   92

15. SOUL THAT CAME TO QUENCH ITS THIRST   101

16. INHERITED VENDETTA: A TALE OF RETRIBUTION   107

Contents

17. SINISTER HAUNTS: A VENGEFUL HIGHWAY
    SPECTRE   117

About The Author

Shri Jayaraj Menon, having retired from the Central Government under the Finance Ministry after over three decades of service, has delved into his second literary work, "The Nightmare Chronicles." This comes after his initial book, "My Memoirs," a reflective piece covering his life journey from childhood to retirement. In this new book, the author explores an entirely different subject, skillfully compiling various strange real-life incidents that unfolded in different phases of his life. He narrates these stories ingeniously, presenting them in a subtle manner that captivates readers, fostering a sense of compulsive reading. While certain incidents may seem to defy logic, the author acknowledges the existence of many phenomena that elude scientific explanation. The language is simple, the narration is free-flowing, and readers are likely to find resonance with some incidents in their own lives. Grounded in real-life experiences, the book promises a gratifying reading experience.

Preface

After the overwhelming response to my first book, 'My Memoirs,' a compilation of personal reflections that resonated with both relatives and friends in a good measure, I found myself compelled to embark on a new literary venture. This time, I sought to delve into the realm of the supernatural—unveiling a collection of real-life stories featuring ghosts, spirits, and certain weird incidents that I had personally witnessed or encountered in my life. These narratives, though integral to my life story, lingered in my thoughts for years but remained untold in 'My Memoirs' due to various constraints. The dormant idea only needed a spark of inspiration to come to life, and that inspiration came in the form of the enthusiastic feedback I received after my first book.

This book stands as a testament to the encouragement and support I received from my loved ones, propelling me to lay bare these intriguing tales. Within these pages lie accounts of eerie occurrences that challenge the notion that our world is solely inhabited by the living. Spirits and intangible beings, it seems, may share our existence, offering an unseen company that transcends the boundaries of the tangible.

As I navigate my retirement days, I view this project as a creative endeavour to share my experiences in simple, truthful language. The tales recounted within are rooted in reality, though the mind, perhaps influenced by a touch of hallucination, may have shaped the perception of these encounters.

This collection of real-life ghost stories not only invites you to accompany me on a journey into the mysterious and unexplained but also provides an opportunity for you, the reader, to engage with your own perspective. The intention is not just to entertain but also to educate and explore the cultural significance of these ghostly narratives. I believe that many readers may have encountered similar incidents in their own lives—whether in childhood, family traditions, or events that sparked their interest in the paranormal.

So, with an open mind and a curious spirit, I invite you to join me on this exploration through the captivating stories that unfold within these pages. Together, let us navigate the shadowy realms and form our own opinions on the supernatural mysteries that inhabit our world.

Jayaraj Menon
Belapur, Navi Mumbai
January 2024

CHAPTER ONE

HAUNTED HIGH NOON: AYYAPPAN OR THE TRICKSTER SPIRIT OF KORAPPAN?

My reflections on our ancestral home vividly revolved around the memorable moments from our childhood, spent amidst the reassuring presence of our dear grandmother. As the matriarch and guiding force of our extensive family, she served as the pillar of strength for all of us. In our generation, none of us had the fortune to meet our grandfather, so our grandmother was our source of energy and sustenance.

The enormous size of our family ensured a perpetually lively atmosphere, with numerous cousins turning our home into a hub of joy and fun. Vacation times held a special charm, and occasional visits from distantly located cousins added a unique flavour to our days. Days were filled with outdoor adventures, from impromptu treasure hunts both inside and outside the house to spirited games of tag. The vacation time in the ancestral house became a cherished memory, a time when the echoes of laughter and the warmth of family ties left an indelible mark on the hearts of all involved.

The approach road in front of the house, the two bathing ponds to the north and south, and a small stretch of paddy fields at the rear still remain etched in my memory. The low-level branches of the solitary mango tree, gracefully leaning over the paddy fields, were a great place for all of us to spend time in the evenings. The tree would be unusually crowded, especially during hot afternoons, as we sat and watched the labourers toil in the sun-soaked fields. Once the harvest season was over and the fields lay barren, the space was turned into a football ground, where we often engaged in spirited matches with our neighbour Alavi and his younger brother Hameed.

Ayyappan, one of the trusted domestic helps of our grandmother, hung swings from the mango tree's branches, providing never ending amusement as we took turns swinging. Valiyamma's (mother's elder sister) daughter, Devi Eduthy, led our pack as our undisputed leader, guiding us in both outdoor and indoor games, while her younger sister, Radheduthy, played second fiddle to her, and both of them formed the nucleus of our bubbling band of mischief mongers. When the sun reached its zenith and its rays became too harsh to endure, we sought refuge indoors, engaging ourselves in card games, ludo, snake & ladder, and various other absorbing indoor activities.

During one such summer vacation, as usual, we were engaged in a dice game. I suffered an early defeat, followed by Devi Eduthy. Knowing well that it would be a while before we would get another turn, given the rule that the winner would be the one who knocked everyone else out of the game, I realized it would take more than an hour for the game to end due to the number of players involved. While Devi Eduthy went to take a nap, I chose to step outside onto the main road and spend some time there, as I didn't want to merely sit in the group as an onlooker and watch others play.

I made my way to the main road, which lay approximately 100 meters from our front courtyard, and sat down under the shade of two large trees—a favourite hangout for us in the evenings.

Interestingly, the two big trees a mango and a banyan, grew conjoined, their trunks fused with each other, giving the impression from a distance that they were one. Just in front of me, a culvert passed under the road. Across the road there was a small hill, overlooking the main road. Sitting beneath the twin trees, I looked up at the unfrequented hill, which seemed devoid of any signs of life. The afternoon was exceedingly hot, with the sun emitting intense heat waves from all sides. At home all the adults were blissfully revelling in a well-deserved siesta.

There wasn't a single person in sight anywhere nearby. Only a couple of bus services operated on this stretch of road: the BMS from Kuttippuram to Guruvayur and the TMS between Ponani and Pattambi. During the midnoon hours, their services came to a standstill. The place was incredibly peaceful, with the soft swirling sounds of leaves in the gentle breeze breaking the silence occasionally. Slowly, I stretched out my legs and comfortably fitted myself in the space between the two large protruding roots of the trees. The mild breeze blowing across provided some relief from the scorching sun's heat, and I lay there, lost in my thoughts, until a tap on my shoulder abruptly pulled me from my reverie.

Turning around, I found Ayyappan, standing in front, as usual, wearing a warm and toothless grin. He inquired what I was doing under the twin trees all by myself. I did not say anything but gave him a broad smile. I had seen him smoking a beedi covertly behind the cowshed as I walked onto the road, but he was wearing a different attire then.

Ayyappan said he was heading to the Parakkulam hills to meet a friend and asked if I wanted to join him. I was very excited as I had never been to Parakkulam hills before. It felt like a once-in-a-lifetime opportunity to explore a new place, although thoughts of the impending game at home made me a bit hesitant. But Ayyappan assured me that we would be back in an hour, and his gentle, persistent persuasion eventually provided the spark needed to ignite my enthusiasm.

As I walked alongside Ayyappan in the scorching sun, the heat of the road seared beneath my bare feet. Ayyappan, appeared unperturbed by the melting asphalt, avidly described the attractions of the hill — numerous gooseberry trees and a shallow well with cool, refreshing water. The anticipation within me grew by leaps and bounds, and I couldn't wait to reach the hills. After a brisk fifteen-minute walk, we finally reached the base of the hill.

The hilltop glistened under the relentless sun, blazing high in the clear, blue sky. On the summit, the heat intensified, baking the hill's surface into a dry and arid landscape. Vegetation was sparse, struggling to thrive in the unforgiving conditions. Only a few tenacious plants and shrubs managed to survive, their leaves wilting and curling under the unrelenting heat. Seeking relief, I quickly located a large mango tree and sought refuge under its shade. The hilltop offered a breathtaking view, showcasing a panoramic vista of the surrounding landscape. In the distance, the horizon dazzled in the heat, creating a mirage-like effect.

Ayyappan asked me to follow him to the rear side of the hill, where he showed me a cluster of gooseberry trees laden with big ripe berries. Quickly, I clambered onto one of them and plucked a handful of berries. They had a delightful sweet and tangy taste, and I relished them sitting on its branch. After enjoying a few, I got down and asked Ayyappan to take me to the well that supposedly had very sweet water in it. He led me to the well, but it was relatively deep, with the level of water only a few feet from the bottom. The well appeared to be in disuse for ages, and I wondered how I would be able to draw water from it without the help of a rope, bucket, and pulley.

Ayyappan had an answer for that. Leaving me there, he went to fetch a rope and a makeshift bucket made of 'paala' (leaf of the areca nut tree) from one of his acquaintances. As Ayyappan disappeared from sight, I wanted to take another look into the depths of the well. Leaning over its edge, I saw my own reflection in the blue water. I picked up a few small stones and threw them into the water one by one. I observed as my reflection distorted in the ripples created by the stones. A few minutes later, I heard the sound of footsteps behind me, and I thought Ayyappan had returned. Before I could turn around to see, a hard push sent me hurtling down into the well. I fell into the water with a loud splash, narrowly escaping from hitting the inner rings of the well. Struggling to stay afloat, I called out for Ayyappan. My desperate cries from the dark abyss echoed within, unable to reach Ayyappan, who seemed to be away from the place—or so it appeared.

Terribly shaken and frightened, I tried to cling to a few runners of wild plants growing inside the well. The blue sky presented a picture of the ferocious sun blazing away above. The circular inner rings around the girth of the well were surrounded by wild vegetation, indicating that it hadn't been in regular use for many years. This realization heightened my apprehension. Tales of snakes inhabiting such thick undergrowth came to my mind, and I feared the worst. I regretted my decision to accompany Ayyappan to this forsaken place, but dwelling on the past was futile; I was now caught in a dire situation, and finding a way to extricate myself was my immediate priority.

Regaining my composure quickly I attempted to clamber up the well by grabbing onto the wild plants growing along its walls. It was a strenuous struggle, but somehow, I managed to make my way up. By the time I reached the top, I was utterly exhausted. With one final lunge forward, I propelled myself out of the well and slumped on the ground, lying motionless there for several moments before slipping into unconsciousness.

Hours seemed to pass and suddenly I felt a splash of water on my face, rousing me from my unconscious state. The splash of water made me believe that I was still in the well. Opening my eyes, I found myself lying on my grandmother's bed, with her sitting nearby, wearing a concerned expression. My mother and valiyamma were also standing by her side. Grandmother questioned why I had made the reckless visit to Parakkulam hill alone, especially in the scorching sun. Then I narrated the entire sequence of events to her, explaining how Ayyappan had coerced me into following him there.

To my surprise, all of them had amused smiles on their faces as they listened to my story. A smiling valiyamma told me that Ayyappan had been working in the backyard throughout the afternoon, clearing the clogged furrows with a spade. My mother recalled seeing him sitting on the backside veranda around that time, drinking water from the earthen pot placed near the steps. Grandmother also confirmed his presence, having heard him talking to someone from near her bedroom window while she was taking a nap. It became clear to them that there was something incongruous in my version of the story, and I was trying to mislead them into believing that it was Ayyappan who had taken me to that remote place in the scorching sun, pushing me into the wretched well. They suspected I was hiding something from them, fearing the wrath of the elders, as it could never have been Ayyappan.

Feeling dejected as nobody believed me, I looked out and spotted Ayyappan standing outside by the side of the window, glancing at me. His trademark toothless smile and the mischievous glint in his eyes now made me terribly uneasy. Before moving away, he gave me a sly wink, and I hastily turned my head away from him. Nevertheless, the thought hounded me as I tried to figure out if it was not Ayyappan, who could it have been. However, my mind was firm in its belief that the person who shepherded me to the Parakkulam hills was none other than our own Ayyappan.

Later, my mother revealed to me that a group of men found me in an unconscious state, lying near the well, while returning from their prayers at a nearby mosque. Luckily, one of them recognized me, as I used to buy candies from his shop off and on. He also knew which house I belonged to, so they carried me home safely.

Days and months passed, and I kept pestering Ayyappan to come clean about the incident, but he consistently evaded giving me a definite answer, responding only with an enigmatic smile. Then, one late evening when I was returning from a shop, I met Ayyappan on the way. He appeared in an inebriated state, terribly wobbling as he walked. Standing in front of me, he, in an unsteady stutter, asked if I genuinely wished to know the truth about the incident that had happened at Parakkulam hills a few months ago. In my eagerness to uncover the truth and redeem my pride by proving that it wasn't a fabricated story, I urged him to go ahead and spill the beans.

Ayyappan squatted on a nearby roadside milestone and began to speak haltingly. The familiar glint in his eyes had disappeared, replaced by an expression of sorrow. He revealed that he had a twin brother, Korappan, who looked exactly like him, but God was not kind enough to let him live long in this world. Korappan was a heavy drinker, and an arrack shop near the Parakkulam hills was his favourite meeting place with friends. Eventually, his excessive drinking led to his premature death. Ayyappan then looked skywards, tears streaming down from his eyes. Wiping the tears away, he continued and said it was Korappan who took me to the Parakkulam hills on that day. I was utterly stunned to hear the words of Ayyappan, and a wave of goosebumps covered me from head to toe. The idea seemed incredibly implausible, and I shuddered at the thought of how a deceased man could momentarily return to the world of the living, specifically with the intent to harm another.

It was a harrowing sensation to grapple with the notion of a deceased man lurking in broad daylight, enticing an unsuspecting boy to the Parakkulam hills before pushing him into the abandoned well. Nonetheless, I chose to believe him, acknowledging that alcohol often acted as a truth serum, far more reliable than a polygraph test. Ayyappan continued in his slurred words, recounting that when Korappan was alive, many had mistaken him for Ayyappan, and similar instances had occurred on multiple occasions. Tragically, a couple of boys had fallen victim to Korappan's unsatiated soul, losing their lives in the well.

As he rose and began to depart with an unsteady gait, Ayyappan confessed that on several occasions, he had been apprehended by the local police based on eyewitness accounts linking him to these murder cases. However, our grandmother provided him with an impregnable alibi, asserting that he was at our house when those incidents occurred. The police could not easily disregard her testimony due to her considerable reputation within the locality. Consequently, they had no choice but to absolve him of all charges in those cases. It was his unwavering deference towards grandmother that spared Ayyappan time and again from the clutches of the law.

It appeared that grandmother, mother, and valiyamma were fully cognizant of the enduring presence of Korappan's spirit in the area. Yet, they intentionally pretended to be unaware, aiming to shield the younger generation from being consumed by fear. For me, it was an unforgettable experience to spend some time with a man who had long departed from this world, even though his attempts to draft me into the world he now inhabited, proved unsuccessful. It turned out to be a fortunate escape for me, guided by providence.

CHAPTER TWO

CRYPTIC SHADOWS: 'VENGARA KOTHA'

Our beloved grandmother was a remarkably prominent figure, embodying unparalleled grace and strength in the precious memories of our ancestral home. She was the unshakable bedrock of our family, quietly carrying the weight of our collective well-being on her shoulders. My mother and her elder sister, affectionately addressed as valiyamma by us, ran the household in tandem, with grandmother guiding them all along.

The house always remained a bustling hub, constantly filled with the lively presence of us children, who collectively formed the integral spokes of the giant wheel that was our home. The loyal workforce, commanded by grandmother, added an extra layer of vibrancy and excitement to our days. Many of them possessed a treasure trove of folk tales, which they narrated to us during breaks. Listening to their stories was a terrific experience that I did not wish to miss even once. The dark corridors within the big house and the long stretch of approach road were entwined in a slew of hair-raising stories that they told us, virtually making those places out of bounds for us. Though some of the stories seemed unbelievable, they spurred me into weaving a few of my own, using my imagination. Many a time, my own stories came to haunt me in the night.

The ten-meter-wide muddy stretch of road that connected our front courtyard with the main road figured in many of the folk tales. At its centre, there was a rudimentary wooden gate, consisting of three long bamboo poles horizontally affixed to two sturdy wooden beams on either side. This served as a protective barrier against the entry of stray cattle and other unwanted intruders. During the daytime, it was one of our favourite places to hang out and indulge in some enjoyable pastime. We would spend a lot of time perched on the bamboo poles, performing balancing acts that entertained us no end. However, as night descended, the dark stretch of road and the gate in the middle, changed contours, instilling a great amount of terror among us children. The place then became strictly off-limits for children as all of us knew that on certain specific nights, 'Vengara Kotha' passed through the place and routinely sat on the bamboo poles before moving up the stretch of the approach road to the main road. 'Vengara Kotha' belonged to a tribal community and had been one of the trusted members of our loyal workforce. Sadly, she succumbed to the highly contagious smallpox virus at a very young age.

As children, we were too frightened to go out into the front courtyard at night. However, it appeared that my mother and valiyamma had witnessed the hazy figure of 'Vengara Kotha' many times in the darkness. Seated astride the long bamboo poles, she would gently wave at them while tending to her locks and chewing betel leaves.

If 'Vengara Kotha' spotted our grandmother in the front courtyard, she would take a few measured steps towards our house. Displaying a remarkable degree of courage, our grandmother remained unfazed, closely observing her movements. She always kept a chopper within reach, strategically placed near the bamboo roller blinds in the courtyard. The moment 'Vengara Kotha' advanced a few more steps from the gate, grandmother would take out the chopper and brandish it at her. This served as a potent deterrent, dissuading 'Vengara Kotha' from advancing any further.

After several tense and nail-biting moments, 'Vengara Kotha' would retreat, making her way towards the main road until gradually disappearing into the darkness. The following morning, when we went to the gate to play on the bamboo poles, we found the telltale stain marks of her crimson spittle scattered all across the place. These marks provided undeniable evidence that 'Vengara Kotha' was a tangible reality, not merely a figment of anyone's imagination.

'Vengara Kotha' made similar appearances at one of our bathing ponds located on the northern side of our compound. It was a place seldom visited by anyone during the midday hours. One day, after finishing my lunch, I went around the area looking for fallen ripe mangoes. After collecting a couple of mangoes, I returned home. While returning, I passed by the pond side and distinctly heard the gurgling sounds of water, as if someone was taking a bath in the pond. Eager to know who it was, I went near the pond. To my surprise, there was no one in sight, but I noticed ripples circling on the surface of the water, suggesting that someone had just taken a dip in the water.

I waited patiently for the person to emerge from the depths of the water, while relishing the taste of the mangoes I had in my possession. A few minutes elapsed, yet no one surfaced from the water. But the swirling of ripples continued unabated, creating countless circles of waves on the surface of the water. Suddenly, they intensified, almost forming a vortex and I clearly observed a figure slowly emerging from the depths of the pond. It was a woman with dark skin, adorned with large earrings gently swaying from her earlobes and multiple strands of gleaming bead necklaces draping her otherwise bare front. Her eyes, tinged with crimson, held a fierce gaze as she emerged from the water with a resounding splash. Catching sight of me by the pond, she cast a chilling glance and gestured for me to run away from there. Jolted, I dropped the mangoes there and quickly took to my heels.

When I recounted this incident to my mother, she initially scolded me for wandering around such secluded places at unusual hours. Little later, she explained to me that it was 'Vengara Kotha' whom I had noticed frolicking in the water. 'Vengara Kotha' intentionally chose midday to take a dip in the water, as it was the time when her spectral body felt intolerable heat. When alive, she had bathed in that pond on a few occasions, earning her a stern reprimand from grandmother, who strongly disapproved of outsiders using it. It seemed that in her afterlife, 'Vengara Kotha' was happily indulging in the gratification of all the desires she longed to fulfil while she was alive, fully aware that she now enjoyed complete insulation from admonishment for her actions.

While part of our workforce, 'Vengara Kotha' displayed tremendous loyalty towards our grandmother. Unfortunately, when she died, her mortal remains were denied the proper cremation rites. This tragic situation stemmed from her family's dire poverty and the nature of the disease that claimed her life. Since she had succumbed to fatal smallpox, the hospital authorities refused to release her body to her family, assuming that they might be unable to dispose of the body in a proper manner, leading to a potential widespread infection in the Panchayat from the virus.

What the hospital authorities later did with the corpse was a matter of disgust. Sources at the hospital said that the authorities, following directives from the District Medical Officer (DMO), burnt down the mortal remains in a deplorable manner in an open area using generous amount of acid. It distressingly came to the fore that some of her body parts were left half burnt, with scavenging stray dogs feasting on them for several days. In short, the mortal remains of 'Vengara Kotha' were disposed of in a slipshod manner, forgoing the customary Hindu rituals.

Grandmother was deeply agitated by the apathy shown by the District Medical Officer (DMO) and the hospital staff. She sent her chief domestic help to summon the Panchayat President home and expressed her displeasure in no uncertain terms. However, by then, it was too late, and the remains of 'Vengara Kotha's' body had been eaten away by stray dogs, rendering retrieval an impossible task. Grandmother had wished for 'Vengara Kotha's' soul to find peace, no matter where it had departed to, but she had to eventually come to terms with the unfortunate turn of events.

It was the firm belief of Grandmother that neglecting post-death rituals could lead to the soul wandering aimlessly in this world. She was convinced that due to 'Vengara Kotha's unstinted affection for our household, her spirit frequently made its presence felt within our boundaries, as her restless soul continued its quest for salvation.

CHAPTER THREE

TRYST WITH THE LURKING SOULS OF ARAKKAL GRAVEYARD

After the disbandment of the Indian National Army following Indian independence and my father's discharge from service in his prime, he established his home at Palat in a small village called Kumaranallur. We spent a major part of our childhood there. However, after my paternal grandmother passed away from old age, my mother moved with the four of us to stay with her mother at our ancestral house in Padinjarangadi, leaving my father to plough a lone furrow at Palat. My father maintained an excellent relationship with our grandmother, and he came to our ancestral house occasionally to visit her.

One evening, my father came to our ancestral home to attend a function. The event unexpectedly extended well beyond its expected duration, leading to dinner being served close to midnight. After the conclusion of the event, as father prepared to leave for Palat, both my mother and grandmother urged him to stay back and leave the following morning. They were concerned about his late-night two-kilometre walk back to Kumaranallur. However, he was firm in his decision, undeterred by the distance and the late hour.

As he put on his sandals and stepped out of the house, father turned around and casually asked me if I wanted to accompany him. This unexpected invitation took me by surprise, and without any hesitation, I readily agreed. It was a spontaneous decision on my part, and the prospect of walking those two kilometres in the dark of night didn't bother me at all. I craved for a change of location after spending many days in succession at our ancestral house. The disapproving expressions on my mother and grandmother's faces couldn't rein me in, and without a flashlight in hand, my father and I began our walk, melting into the darkness that welcomed us on our way towards Palat.

We went past the muddy path that extended from the front courtyard of our ancestral house to the main road, guided by the soft radiance of the dark clouds overhead. It seemed that the moon was shy of making its appearance, and in its absence, the stars above shimmered brilliantly, their benign luminance creating a silver pathway that we could tread with assurance. Along the main road, the tall 'pala' tree (Jack tree) stood like a silent guardian. The swishing sound of its leaves in the gentle breeze broke the pervasive silence. This 'pala' tree had been at the centre of many fairy tales, the kind that sent shivers down the spine, adding a spooky aura to our nightly journey.

I had heard a few terrifying stories about bewitching witches, attired in flowing white saris, haunting the shadows of the 'pala' tree. People who ventured around the area at odd hours in the night often found themselves entranced by the mesmerizing presence of these weird beings. The witches would halt these unsuspecting wanderers in their tracks, requesting lime to apply to their betel leaves and those who paused to accede to their request, unable to resist their beguiling looks, met a terrible fate. Their remains were discovered the next morning, perched atop the nearby palm trees in a grim pile of bones and skulls.

While father walked briskly, I struggled to keep up with his pace. I was determined to walk as close to him as possible, not wanting to leave an inch of space between us, and to prevent the fear factor from gnawing at my mind in the pitch darkness. Perhaps sensing my unease, my father struck up a conversation to alleviate it. His presence was immensely reassuring, and I made an effort to calm my nerves, pushing the scary tales of the 'pala' tree and bloodthirsty witches to the back of my mind.

Soon, we reached the intersection at Engineer Road, marking the halfway point to Kumaranallur. The road sloped down, winding past the famous 'Arakkal' mosque, located beside a vast burial ground. As we continued our brisk walk, going past a curve along the meandering road, I heard faint footsteps of someone closely following us. It felt as though we had a companion, right behind us. My father, too, appeared to have sensed the same. In a hushed tone he advised me to keep moving forward without looking back, and we continued without breaking our stride.

The footsteps became swifter, as if someone or something were rapidly closing in on us. Tension gripped me, and my heart pulsated heavily within my chest. Amid my escalating panic, I heard my father's reassuring whisper. He kept on urging me not to look back and to remain calm. His firm grip on my hand infused me with much more courage, acting as a lifeline in the darkness, shielding me from the approaching threat.

We continued to walk with the sound of footsteps following us in close pursuit. My father always carried a Malappuram knife securely sheathed on his belt as a safety measure whenever he ventured out at night. I had observed him discreetly ensuring it was very much in place by running his right palm over his shirt a little while ago. I knew he was dauntlessly brave, exceptionally strong, and had received extensive hand-to-hand combat training during his days in the Indian National Army. As long as he was by my side, I felt an overpowering feeling of security. However, my heart refused to trust my conscience and pounded away rapidly within my chest. The road ahead seemed to stretch on interminably. The footsteps now approached uncomfortably closer, and I feared that someone might strike us from behind with a heavy object. I thought the end was imminent and glanced at my father in real concern. He appeared calm, treading his steps carefully, as if he were readying himself for some action. A couple of minutes passed, and gradually, the sound of the footsteps faded before falling completely silent, like a distant sound dissipating into nothingness.

As we moved on, my father explained certain beliefs related to souls that hadn't attained spiritual salvation after death, causing them to hang around burial grounds. These restless spirits were thought to be caught in a liminal space between the domain of the living and the afterlife. According to him, these spirits were believed to attempt to make contact with the living, often driven by the intent to fulfil unfinished desires and wishes.

He went on to tell that there were age-old beliefs suggesting that these discontented souls might even attempt to possess the bodies of the living. The rationale behind this was to find a temporary refuge that allowed them to experience the physical world once more. They seemed to prefer the bodies of the weak-hearted, as these individuals were more susceptible to their unsolicited entry. This was precisely why my father asked me not to look back or panic, urging me to keep moving forward.

Though these concepts were demanding for me to grasp, I listened to my father's explanations with rapt attention. After a few minutes, we reached home, and my breathing returned to a normal rhythm. As I lay beside my father on the bed, I wondered if any disgruntled soul had somehow managed to force its way into my body in a brief moment of fear taking over me, and how I would behave the following morning if it did. However, everything appeared normal when I woke up the next day.

CHAPTER FOUR

TIPPU AND THE EXORCIST

Within the vast expanse of our ancestral house, our grandmother maintained a small herd of cattle that played crucial roles in various aspects of our daily lives. The bullocks formed an integral part of her empire, serving essential functions such as ploughing and tilling the agricultural land, while the well-bred cows ensured a consistent and reliable supply of milk for our family. Grandmother spared no effort in ensuring the well-being of her bovine force, and to address the diverse needs of these animals, she had dedicated men in service whose responsibility was to take care of the needs of the herd.

Our eldest cousin, affectionately called Ettan, took on the responsibility of overseeing all the household affairs, which included managing both the livestock and the labour force. In addition to these duties, he also successfully operated a ration shop, managing these responsibilities proficiently.

One day Ettan brought home a lovely biscuit-coloured puppy named Tippu. He belonged to a local breed and became the heir apparent to his predecessor, Tommy, who had been a loyal member of our family since our childhood until he passed away due to old age. Tippu was a friendly and obedient dog when it came to his master, Ettan, but he didn't extend the same disposition to others.

Over time, Tippu developed a bitter animosity towards me, possibly due to my occasional teasing, leading to an ongoing resentment between us. One day, it escalated into a brief but intense conflict during which Tippu managed to prise off a small chunk of flesh from my right thigh with his razor-sharp canines. While my trousers failed miserably to offer any protection, the blood that gushed from the wound painted them red in anger.

Sensing severe ramifications, Tippu did not stay a minute longer and ran away from home. Even as darkness fell, he did not return. Following grandmother's instructions, our dedicated workforce embarked on a quest to find the elusive Tippu, scrupulously searching every likely hideout. Nursing my thigh wound, I also joined them in the search operations. Despite our zealous efforts, there was no trace of Tippu to be found. The search operations continued late into the night, but Tippu remained untraceable. Days turned into weeks, and no matter how hard we tried, Tippu didn't come back. Everyone at home, including myself, was sad and deeply anguished. His disappearance had softened my enmity towards him.

A whole month passed, and we were gradually coming to terms with the reality of living without Tippu in our midst. However, one early morning, Ettan heard a soft growl at the front door of our house. When he opened the door, to our surprise and delight, there was Tippu, wagging his tail incessantly. He appeared gaunt and cadaverous; his eyes devoid of the sparkle they once had. All of us gathered around Tippu as he showered us with affectionate licks. This was an unusual trait for Tippu, and I happily wondered if he had changed. Tears of pure joy streamed down from our eyes. It was a glorious morning for all of us, as our beloved companion, who had been missing for so long, had returned to where he belonged.

As our initial excitement waned, we began to notice a queer expression in his eyes, hinting at underlying discomfort over the next few days. His behaviour gradually shifted from being friendly and diffident to something anomalous and strange. This transformation continued for weeks, and it became evident that

Tippu was no longer the same friendly dog, he once was. He always remained in a reflective mood, going through his daily routines mechanically. He first lost his appetite and thirst, and after a few days he stopped eating altogether. This was a matter of serious concern for us.

Expressing serious concern, grandmother urged Ettan to seek the advice of a veterinary practitioner immediately. During this time, one of our acquaintances had happened to see Tippu, and after observing his eyes, he hypothesized that Tippu was under the influence of an evil spirit. He suspected that a malignant spirit could have possessed Tippu during his time away from home and advised that someone versed in paranormal topics be consulted to restore Tippu back to normalcy. Meanwhile, rumors began circulating that Tippu was possibly under the influence of demonic possession.

Using his broad network of contacts, Ettan got in touch with a local exorcist—someone with the expertise and capability to perform the necessary incantations to evict the foul entity believed to have possessed Tippu. After obtaining grandmother's assent, a date was set to bring him home.

On a lazy evening, as I returned from school, an unusual ruckus drew my attention near the cowshed where Tippu was kept on a leash. Seeing the unusual gathering around Tippu, I tossed my school bag onto the porch and dashed towards the scene. There, I spotted an elderly man in a squatting position engaged in performing a ritual in front of Tippu. Flanking him were Ettan, our domestic help, Ayyappan, and a couple of unknown individuals. A plantain leaf was placed by the side of the man, containing flowers, turmeric powder, an ambiguous dark substance—possibly burnt husk—and a black thread with multiple knots. I presumed he was the exorcist, expected to free Tippu from the evil spirit that had possessed him.

Evidently displeased Tippu watched the proceedings with a bewildered look, occasionally trying to free himself from his restraints. A muzzle was placed over his mouth, presumably to prevent him from barking and biting. Tippu's front legs were tightly held by Ayyappan, preventing him breaking away. The muffled growls of Tippu created a lot of unease within me. The stark helplessness reflecting in his eyes made me feel that human beings were more insentient than animals. I wanted to set him free, but the sight of Ettan's bloodshot eyes and his twirled-up moustache nipped the thought in the bud.

Despite all the weird things that happened around him, Tippu looked adorable with a dab of scarlet vermilion on his forehead and a floral garland around the neck. The exorcist mumbled some mantras incoherently and made strange gestures with his hands, a mystifying performance that left my young mind dismayed. This peculiar ritual lasted about ten minutes before he produced a handful of ash from his cloth pouch.

With a swift and unexpected motion, he hurled a bit of ash on the face of Tippu. Startled and incensed, Tippu leapt at the exorcist, the leash holding him in check, sparing him from certain harm. Unmindful of the belligerent actions of Tippu, the exorcist reached into his cloth pouch once again and pulled out a small earthen pot. He instructed one of his assistants to remove the muzzle from Tippu's mouth and carefully force it open. He then poured a potion from the pot into Tippu's mouth which the distressed puppy had no choice but to swallow under duress. About a minute later, Tippu started to twirl on his leash before collapsing on the ground like a wooden log. A frothy liquid trickled from his mouth, and with his half-closed eyes, he lay on the ground listlessly.

The exorcist then produced a nail and hammer from his pouch. The sight of them made my knees shatter in fright. I heard him tell Ettan that the nail would be driven into Tippu's front paw for a brief moment before being carefully removed. It was essential to extract a drop of Tippu's purportedly contaminated blood to be presented as an offering to the demonic spirits of the cosmic world. After this ritual, Tippu would return to his normal self. A sudden anguish enveloped me as I shuddered at the thought of the impending horror.

The exorcist assured Ettan that the blood-drawing process wouldn't cause any pain to Tippu because the concoction he had administered down Tippu's throat was a sedative. Reluctantly, Ettan consented to this distressing act. My heart pounded with a blend of fright and anger. I cast a fervent glance at Ettan, urging him to intervene and prevent the exorcist from subjecting the hapless canine to such a painful ordeal. Once again, the sight of his imposing moustache and fear-inducing red eyes halted me, leaving me to watch the proceedings helplessly.

Acting on the directions of the master, his assistant straightened Tippu's front leg and held his paw firmly pinned to the ground. Tippu lay in a benumbed state under the influence of the sedative, oblivious to what was about to befall him. The exorcist carefully positioned the nail at the centre of Tippu's tender right paw, and wielding the hammer, he was all set to strike. As he raised the hammer, I found myself unable to bear witness to the imminent act of cruelty and began sobbing uncontrollably. Ettan held my hands firmly, shielding my eyes by cupping them with his palms. In that harrowing moment, just as the hammer was about to come down with a resounding thud, I summoned all my strength and broke free from Ettan's grasp. While doing so, my hands collided hard on something, and that produced a loud shriek. It was not the yelping of Tippu but the agonised scream of what appeared to be a boy in excruciating pain.

Instantaneously a stinging smack landed on my cheek, forcing me to open my eyes. To my bewilderment, neither Tippu nor the exorcist were in sight. Instead, I found myself on the bed, with Sivettan, my elder brother, sitting up beside me, vigorously rubbing his forehead. It suddenly struck me that the scream I heard was of Sivettan, and the object I thought I had inadvertently struck while freeing myself from Ettan's clutches was his forehead. The slap I received in return was a reflexive reaction from him that brought me back to my senses.

CHAPTER FIVE

'POTTI' THE MISCHIEVOUS SPIRIT

In the lap of the Vellaloor hills, far removed from the noise and tumult of our bustling village life, stood the only ancient Shiva temple in our locality. Time had not been kind to this temple, as it had fallen into a state of absolute ruins due to the neglect of the local residents. However in recent times, a remarkable transformation had taken place, breathing new life into its weathered stones. The restoration of this temple was a massive undertaking, a testament to the strong unity of the nearby Hindu households. A group of determined young men, deeply devoted to their faith, came together selflessly to renovate this sacred place. Over the next several months, they worked tirelessly, facing the elements and overcoming numerous obstacles to complete the task they had undertaken.

Now, as the sun bathed the Vellaloor hills in its warm rays, the Shiva temple looked majestic, no longer a relic of the past but a vibrant symbol of steadfast faith and the resilient spirit of a community that refused to let its sacred heritage fade into obscurity. After the temple's renovation, it began to draw a regular flow of devotees from nearby villages every day. The regular evening poojas were conducted under the sponsorship of the nearby households in our locality, and this tradition continued without interruption. The responsibility of sponsoring the poojas fell on our household once every month, and it was my mother and I who went to the temple on that day with all the requisite articles. I derived immense pleasure from accompanying my mother wherever she went, playfully earning the sobriquet 'the tail of mother' within our immediate family—a label I had no qualms about shaking off.

Once, our turn fell on a Friday, and my mother had made all the preparations to go to the temple well before I returned from school. As the sun dipped below the horizon, painting the sky with shades of orange and pink, we set out from home for the temple. It was a half-hour trek along the bunds of the vast paddy fields, through the rugged terrains of the Vellaloor hills, and I steadfastly followed in my mother's tracks.

Mother carried our trusty Winchester torch, our beacon to light the way through the dark passages of our return route. Swaying it back and forth, she walked briskly, guiding me forward. On my head, I carried a large brass vessel filled with rice, jaggery, ghee, and various other essential items while holding a bundle of firewood in my hand. This firewood was intended for cooking the payasam, to be offered to the Lord at the conclusion of the pooja. I harboured no bitterness towards carrying the brass vessel on my head and the heavy bundle of firewood in my hand. Such responsibilities were traditionally assigned to the youngest members of the family. My elder brother, Sivettan, deemed it beneath his dignity to carry these ceremonial items to the temple, especially since he was in the high school section at the time. He feared that the prospect of being seen performing such tasks would tarnish his reputation beyond redemption among his peers. However, this weighty task held an added attraction for me, as an extra portion of payasam was on offer as a reward for carrying out this onerous task.

The temple was situated on the rocky terrain of the hillock, and the path to reach it was far from smooth. After an exhausting trek through the vast swathe of paddy fields and craggy alleys, we reached the plains of the Vellaloor hillock. From there, a ten-minute walk along a muddy road brought us to a terrain that ultimately led to the temple compound.

Although I visited the temple once every month, I was amazed each time by the placid surroundings along the way. The gentle breeze sweeping across the paddy fields had wiped away the perspiration, preventing it from trickling into my eyes. However, once we entered the plains, sweat began to flow freely. Struggling to maintain my balance under the weight of the brass vessel on my head and the bundle of firewood in my hand, I repeatedly wiped the sweat away to keep it from obstructing my vision.

The elderly priest was waiting for us at the entrance and warmly greeted us as we arrived at the temple. He promptly took charge of the items I had carried on my head and in my hand. Before heading to the temple kitchen (thidappally) with the materials required for preparing the payasam, he requested that I light all the small metallic lamps positioned around the temple walls.

In half an hour, I completed the task, and the soft radiance of an array of oil lamps embellished the four outer walls of the temple. Their gentle glow flickered in the mild breeze, performing a graceful dance on the temple walls. The pooja began, accompanied by the occasional ringing of a bell and the chanting of sacred mantras resonating from the inner sanctum of the temple. Meanwhile, in the thidappally, a synthesis of rice and jaggery bubbled away, creating lively ripples on the surface of the copper vessel placed over the fire, with a generous amount of ghee kept in a bottle poised to join them in action. The sweet payasam, meant to be offered to Lord Shiva after the pooja, was all set to attain finality. The priest's assistant assiduously stirred the contents of the vessel with a ladle, while the sweet aroma of the simmering porridge filled the precincts of the temple.

A few minutes later, the priest emerged from inside and carried away the steaming hot payasam into the sanctum sanctorum, where he resumed the rituals for a few more minutes in order to sanctify the offering to the deity. At long last, the small doors of the inner sanctum swung open, and the priest emerged, holding the vessel of payasam in his hands. This was the moment I had been eagerly waiting for. Everyone in the temple received a serving of the payasam on small banana leaves as prasadam, while the remaining portion was kept aside for us to take home.

It was time for us to begin our trek back home and we started off with the hot vessel of payasam securely resting on my tiny head. Mother had thoughtfully rolled up a towel and placed it underneath the burning, hot vessel in order to shield my head from its heat. Despite all the discomforts, the alluring aroma of the content inside kept me going. It was nearing 8 p.m., and mother skilfully wielded the Winchester torch to light our way, throwing its powerful beam expertly on the narrow path ahead. After descending from the temple hill and crossing the muddy road, we reached the plains, which resembled a football field with overgrown wild grass on all sides. From the plains, four or five small alleys led in various directions, and we needed to take one of them to make our way towards the paddy fields and eventually reach home.

In the darkness, the entry points to all five alleys seemed identical, making it difficult to find the one we had come from. Relying on her sixth sense, my mother chose the alley that stretched right in front of us. This pathway was narrow covered by the overarching canopy of numerous trees on either side. The ground was carpeted with a layer of withered grass, and the rustling of dry leaves beneath my feet scared me as I walked beside my mother, with one hand holding onto the vessel on my head and the other hand clutching hers tightly. I had a feeling that this was not the path we had taken while coming, and soon it dawned on my mother that we were heading down the wrong path.

The narrow trail took us to an entirely unfamiliar terrain, leaving us utterly confused. We retraced our steps along the same path and then took a different alley from the plains that appeared to be the right one. After a few minutes of striding through the daunting and dimly lit pathway, we found ourselves back at the very spot where the first path had led us. This puzzling cycle continued for nearly half an hour, with each alley we chose leading us to the same exit point. In the bight moonlight, I could clearly see worry written large on mother's face.

We came back to the plains once again and waited there for a while in complete bewilderment, as there was no one to seek guidance from. I found mother deep in contemplation for a moment. After a while, she appeared determined, as if she had discovered the way out. She told me that it was the mischievous spirit 'Potti' trying to trick us. She then asked me to carefully set down the heavy vessel from my head and stay by her side. Handing me the torch, she closed her eyes and assumed a trance-like posture for a couple of minutes, followed by a few minutes of chanting prayers. Then, she turned around three times in circle, fixing her gaze skywards. The moon, which had been hiding behind a cluster of dark clouds, slyly popped up to catch a glimpse of what mother was performing in the darkness, with a bewildered little boy standing by her side. It seemed as though the full moon was thoroughly enjoying mother's antics and winking at us.

At this point, I sensed a change in the make-up of our surroundings, and I thought I glimpsed a dim blue light briefly appearing at the far end before vanishing into thin air. Perhaps mother also sighted the same light and with great elation told me it was the correct path to head back home. The moon shone brightly, dispelling its diffidence, giving us the feeling that it, too, was part of the sinister plot orchestrated by 'Potti' to mislead us in such an isolated place at night.

Mother led the way as we resumed our journey homeward. Heaving the heavy vessel back onto my head, I followed her closely. I walked right behind mother as she waved the torch back and forth, providing enough light to guide our way. The winding alley eventually brought us to the vast, sweeping paddy fields, and within fifteen minutes, we reached home.

During our walk back home, I asked my mother to tell me more about the mischievous spirit 'Potti' and why it was attempting to confuse us in finding our way. She explained to me that 'Potti' was a disembodied spirit with impish designs to trick or confuse pedestrians' sense of direction, especially at night. She told me about many fascinating beliefs found in various cultures and folklore. In these diverse traditions, mystic entities often tempted travellers away from their intended paths, leaving them lost in unfamiliar terrain. These invisible beings were generally harmless and had different names and characteristics in various regions. In some regions, they were referred to as wisp ghosts, fated to wander aimlessly, holding lanterns at night. But she was not sure about the etymological origin of the term 'Potti.'

The explanations provided by mother generated even more interest in me, and I asked her how she managed to break free from the illusionary web of 'Potti' and find our way back home. She then recited a sacred mantra to me, one that had been passed down through generations and which she had learned from her own mother. It was a powerful incantation known for warding off such mischievous and invisible spirits.

While sleeping at night, these thoughts came unsolicited into my mind. I believed that the world we inhabited was teeming with a multitude of spirits, both in tangible and intangible manifestations. I realised that among them, some were innocuous and caused no apparent harm, while a few others were obliquely spiteful and malicious. The mere notion of these spirits coexisting in the same space as we do, persistently seeking to haunt us from every conceivable corner, left me feeling jittery. It seemed wise to keep oneself away from their prying eyes as best as possible, but in reality, it proved to be a formidable challenge. Closing my eyes, I attempted to shake off these thoughts and find restful sleep.

CHAPTER SIX

THE EERIE CAVERNS OF NARIMALAN KUNNU

The staggering hillock, known as Narimalan Kunnu, amidst vast expanses of paddy fields, had been a prominent landmark of our modest village. It exuded an air of mystery and trepidation, deterring many villagers from approaching it. As school-going children, we had heard from some of our peers that it was an excellent retreat destination, boasting an abundance of gooseberry trees, a vast open ground—twice the size of our school's playground—and a few caves with intriguing historical connections. Since nobody had firsthand information about the hill, it remained as hearsay.

Despite its grandeur, it remained an enigma, shrouded in mysteries yearning to be uncovered. The deep caves and the impressions of massive footprints hinted that colossal beings might have once traversed the gleaming, lumpy rocks gracing the hill's summit. As a curious child, I frequently stared at it from a distance, captivated by the concealed secrets it harboured.

Determined not to be daunted by the scare of exploring the hill, my friends Balakrishnan, Sivarama Das, Abdul Razak, Deepak Kumar (Deepu), Raj Govind, and I decided to undertake an expedition to the awe-inspiring Narimalan Kunnu. We meticulously planned our adventure trip for a Friday afternoon, as this particular day provided an additional hour of recess to enable Muslim students to visit the mosque for prayers. Taking full advantage of this Friday benevolence, we, a pack of adventurers brimming with excitement and eagerness to conquer the summit of a hillock, gathered at the hill's base after hastily finishing our lunches.

The day was sweltering and muggy, yet it failed to dampen our spirits. It took us nearly twenty minutes to cross the pitted terrain and reach the summit of the hill. On reaching the peak, we were enthralled by the breathtaking panorama, which showcased not only the spectacular view from the hilltop of our village but also the surrounding landscapes of Anakkara and Kalladathur. At the pinnacle of the hill, we stumbled upon a treasure trove of gooseberry trees clustered together and an enormous playground that seemed to beckon us to revel on its surface. While the playground appeared unused for ages, the tall grass that grew on its sides provided an attractive sight.

As we continued our exploration, we saw several massive footprints resembling those of abnormal human beings imprinted on the surface of the rugged rocks. According to local folklore, after their twelve-year exile in the forests, the Pandavas had to live in disguise for an additional year. During this period of living incognito, they happened to visit this hill briefly. The belief was that the huge footprints belonged to none other than Bheem, one of the Pandavas.

We continued our exploration around the peak of the hill, and on one side, we discovered the three creepy caves that the villagers had spoken about with an element of apprehension. These caverns were dark inside and emitted a pungent odour. To our amazement, when we hurled a few stones into the caves, a cloud of bats darted out, making screeching sounds as they flew around the place in disarray. We had learned in our class that bats had poor eyesight during the daytime and relied on echolocation through high-frequency sounds they emitted to determine their flight path. They mostly rested in their hideouts during the daytime and ventured out only under the cover of darkness. This odyssey also acted as a kind of study tour for us, allowing us to observe the life patterns of bats firsthand, adding an unexpected twist to our adventure.

When the harsh sun rays proved too hot to handle, we assembled under a gooseberry tree. Bunches of zesty berries tempted us from the treetops. A few of us climbed the trees to pluck a handful of these juicy berries. Sitting in the shade, we relished the sweet and tangy taste of the berries. It was now time for us to indulge in a game of football, one of the top priorities of our mission. We still had half an hour before our classes resumed after recess, and even if we were late by a few minutes, it did not matter since the class that followed after the recess was Hindi, a subject disliked by all of us.

Six of us formed two teams, each consisting of three members. The playing field on the hilltop was a stinging turf, with sharp stones protruding all across its surface. The ground itself radiated a searing heat under the relentless sun. Despite the demanding conditions, we managed to engage in an exhilarating game that lasted a good half an hour.

Towards the end of our spirited match, a shot inadvertently sent the ball soaring into one of the caves. Scores of bats, expressing their displeasure at our action, flew out helter-skelter in all directions. With a mix of curiosity and apprehension, we approached the cave entrance cautiously.

The ball remained hidden from our view outside, and we suspected it might have bounced off the sharp, resilient walls, sending it rolling deeper into the dark cavern. We sat in a huddle near the mouth of the cave for some time, braving the unpleasant stench that continued to emanate from its depths. The ball held significant value for us, so leaving it behind was not an option. However, the pressing question that weighed on our minds was determining which one of us would be brave enough to venture into the cave and retrieve the ball.

Soon the deadlock was broken, and the responsibility of retrieving the ball was thrust upon the person whose kick despatched it into the cave. It was Deepu, and he reluctantly agreed, enticed by the promise of a candy from Kunhava's store. With a handkerchief securely tied across his face, Deepu courageously entered the cave. As he trudged deeper inward, more bats fluttered out of the cave. We lost sight of him as he moved further inside. Initially, we could hear the sounds of him shooing away the bats in his path, but soon we lost track of that as well.

As time wore on, increasing concern wrapped us. There was still no sign of Deepu, and no sounds came forth from the depths of the mysterious cavern. For a moment, we deeply regretted sending Deepu inside to retrieve a ball whose value paled in comparison to his safety. The bats, which had been intermittently flying out of the cave, had now terminated their flight operations, heightening our anxiety.

After what felt like an eternity, we could bear the suspense no longer. We called out Deepu's name repeatedly but received no response. Fearful of the unknown dangers lurking inside and the looming consequences, we did not have the courage to enter the cave ourselves and check on him. Brows furrowed with worry, sweat trickled down our faces, and soon, helplessness prevailed over all of us. Left with no alternative, we ran back to school to report the matter to our class teacher as quickly as possible.

Back in school, we hurriedly stormed into the staffroom to meet our class teacher, Thankamani Madam. She was not there, but we found her engaged in a conversation with the headmaster, M. T. Govindan Nair sir, in the passage of the adjacent building. We ran to them and, regaining our breath quickly, reported every detail about our visit to Narimalan Kunnu and the subsequent incident of sending Deepu into the cave to retrieve our lost ball. The headmaster and Thankamani Madam appeared very concerned when we informed them that Deepu was still trapped inside the cave, even after a significant amount of time had passed since he entered it.

The headmaster immediately called upon his most trusted teachers and instructed them to rush to the hilltop to extricate Deepu from the cave safe and sound. The teachers promptly galvanised all the peons for assistance, and, led by the most dependable Raman, they sprang into action, dashing towards the hill. On hearing about Deepu's predicament, many other students joined us, and within fifteen minutes, we reached the top of the hill.

At the summit of the hill, we guided them to the entrance of the cave where Deepu had disappeared. Our physical education teacher, Velayudhan Nair sir, directed Raman and his junior peons to enter the cave cautiously and locate Deepu. Armed with torches and sticks, Raman and a battery of his companions entered the cavern, cautiously making their way forward. The rest of us waited outside with bated breath, praying for their return with Deepu in good condition.

Time passed at a snail's pace, and suddenly, we could hear Raman's voice echoing from the depths of the cave, announcing that they had found Deepu. He requested that one more person join them to safely extract him. Without dithering for a moment, Velayudhan Nair sir himself volunteered to join the rescue mission. In another ten minutes, all of them came out with smiling faces from the cave, with Deepu cradling in their arms. The constricted passage within the confines of the cave made it tough for them to carry Deepu on their shoulders, but finally they were successful in safely extricating him.

Deepu appeared to be out of his senses as his eyes were closed. They carefully laid him under the shade of a nearby tree. Barring a minor bruise on his forehead, he seemed to be unharmed. Velayudhan Nair sir took out a water bottle from his bag and gently sprinkled a few drops on Deepu's face, which revived him spontaneously. He sat up, gazing around in bewilderment at the onlookers, and soon his emotions overcame him, leading to uncontrollable sobs.

As Deepu struggled to speak, Velayudhan Nair sir provided everyone with a detailed account of what they had seen inside.

The cave was interconnected with another adjacent one, which extended further ahead. The interior was completely shrouded in darkness, and the air inside was stuffy and heavy, contributing to an oppressive atmosphere. A putrid stench of decaying matter hung in the air, making it difficult for them to breathe, and the dearth of fresh oxygen further intensified feelings of discomfort and claustrophobia. Dozens of bats flitted through the darkness, squeaking wildly within the cave, making it difficult for them to move forward to locate Deepu. They found scattered lumps of animal excrement throughout the cave, indicating that certain prowling animals frequented the place, and maybe there were a few hibernating inside. Remnants of half-eaten carcasses within the cave alluded to the presence of predators taking refuge in this desolate hideout. The torch they held in their hands was not particularly effective in those circumstances, so they moved forward by clutching each other's hands, forming a human chain. Eventually, they found Deepu lying unconscious in a corner.

With the assistance of Raman and other peons, Deepu was carried on their shoulders in a procession to the school. On reaching the school, he received a boisterous welcome. Deepu looked cheerful and enjoyed every bit of the reception. He was then taken to the headmaster's room, where he was served tea and biscuits. Velayudhan Nair sir attended to the minor bruise on Deepu's forehead, applying tincture iodine and a soothing ointment. Afterwards, the headmaster requested a senior student who lived near Deepu's house to drop him home on a bicycle.

The headmaster then turned his attention to us, and his menacing glare was an absolute indicator of the brewing disaster. We turned around quickly and plodded our way back to our class. Just as we entered our classroom a peon came running and told us that the headmaster had summoned us to his cabin. Shrivelling in fright, we went back to the headmaster's cabin, expecting a nasty upbraiding from him, accompanied by a few hard canings.

In the cabin, we found our science teacher, Nambeesan sir, busy explaining something to the headmaster, while the head peon,

Raman, was all ears. He was trying to throw light on the probable cause of Deepu losing consciousness inside the cave to the headmaster and attributed it to asphyxiation resulting from a lack of oxygen within the confined space. Perhaps Deepu exacerbated the situation by tying a handkerchief around his nose, further restricting the supply of oxygen to his system. Emphasising that asphyxiation could occur due to choking or inhaling specific chemical substances in claustrophobic conditions, Nambeesan sir, our science teacher, felt the need to offer well-grounded scientific reasoning behind the factors he believed contributed to the incident. Perhaps it was a timely opportunity for him to reaffirm his position as a senior science teacher before the headmaster, especially since there was no one else in the school to validate his findings. However, the monologue, puffed up with conceit, did not appear to have hit the intended target, a conclusion I drew from the expression on the headmaster's face. It also failed to ignite the scientific temper in us; our attention was riveted on the menacing cane of the headmaster resting on his table. The shiny stick seemed ready to launch itself upon our tender palms, leaving indelible imprints for days to come.

When Nambeesan sir wound up his sermon, Raman took over. He narrated a tragic incident that occurred a few years ago when a young boy lost his life in the cave. The parents were unaware that the boy had wandered into the cave, and when he went missing, they searched everywhere except the Narimalan Kunnu. It never occurred to them that the boy might have gone to visit the caves. After a few days, the police arrived and, after gathering some information, discovered the mutilated body of the boy in the cave. A few days after sending the badly mangled corpse for forensic testing and post-mortem, the police concluded that the boy had become a victim of a carnivorous animal in the cave. Subsequently, the police revisited the caves and burst a volley of firecrackers, presumably to drive away animals if any were still holed up inside. They also sprayed some chemicals inside the caves to ward off the menace of scavenging animals from frequenting the place.

However, things once again reverted to the way they were in the earlier days.

As Raman concluded, it was time for the inevitable to happen, and I kept my right palm ready for the eventuality. The headmaster raised his head, his dagger eyes glancing at us piercingly through the thick lenses of his spectacles. Known for his merciless disciplinary methods, we could once again see the dance of death reigning on his deadpan face. We expected no leeway from him this time.

In a moment of surprise and unexpected delight, we beheld a veiled smile grace his face. Never before had we witnessed the headmaster in such a cheerful appearance, allowing us to exhale a collective sigh of relief. Perhaps the scientific reasoning provided to him by the science teacher worked in our favour. Against our initial apprehensions, he let us go with a stern warning and strictly cautioned that a repeat of such irresponsible actions would invite serious consequences. As we left the cabin, he courteously handed us a couple of biscuit packets, apparently procured in honour of Deepu. While departing, I stole a glance at the dejected cane, seemingly squirming on the table, having missed a golden opportunity to assert its might on the tender palms of a few defenceless boys.

Outside the cabin, we met Thangamani Madam. The smiles gracing our relieved faces subtly conveyed to her that the headmaster had granted us a reprieve. But Thangamani Madam was quick to disclose the reason behind this fortunate turn of events. The headmaster's kindness was sparked by a truly auspicious occurrence—a phone call from the District Education Officer, conveying him the happy news that he had been chosen for the Best Headmaster Award in the Ottappalam Educational District. It was this prestigious recognition that led the headmaster to pardon our wrongdoings, paving the way for us to escape unscathed. For once, we felt great admiration for the awards, one of which came to our rescue and saved the blushes for us that day.

CHAPTER SEVEN

ETHEREAL ENIGMA: THE SORCERER AND FORSAKEN HUT

Being born into a large family had its own charms, with one standout being the presence of a lively bunch of cousins. When cousins of all ages gathered at our ancestral house during vacations, it transformed into the epicentre of joy, with round-the-clock merrymaking and gaiety taking place at ground zero. Fortunately, I was born into such a family, and there was never a dearth of amusement or entertainment with a handful of dynamic cousins around.

The scene wasn't any different at 'Palat,' my paternal house, either. During some vacations, my cousin Gopiettan, who lived in Pattambi, would come to stay with us for a change at 'Palat.' He possessed the rare characteristic of entertaining both the young and the old alike, which endeared him to my father. For us, it was always a delight when he made occasional visits home. We were more like buddies, sharing great amity. One of the highlights of his stay was the time we spent in our beautiful bathing pond, reveling for hours, engaging in exhilarating underwater pranks, and catching water snakes with improvised lassos.

During one of his visits, we went to watch a football match in Edappal, a town about 7 kilometers away from our village. The match turned out to be quite absorbing, going into extra time and even a penalty shootout. It lasted for so long that by the time it was over, the last bus from Edappal to our village had already left. The situation worsened as the sky turned dark with ominous clouds. With no other options available, we opted to walk back home, hoping to cover the considerable distance on foot before the heavens opened up.

As we passed the halfway point in Vattamkulam and began descending the slope towards Kuttippala, torrential rains began to lash, accompanied by gusty winds, thunder, and lightning. The road, with no functional streetlights on either side, made it difficult for us to move forward. Adding to the difficulty, the occasional passing vehicles splashed a generous amount of dirty water from the road onto us. This forced us to look for a shelter a little away from the roadside.

We looked around and found a small compound with good tree cover not far from the road. Undaunted by the rain, we ran a steeplechase along the bunds, occasionally tripping into the slushy stretch of paddy fields and jumping across a small canal, finally reaching the open plot of land. Standing beneath a giant tree in the compound and waiting for the rain to lose its bite, I took off my wet shirt, wrung it out, and put it back on. I was about to do the same with my loincloth when I noticed a thatched shed within the compound a few yards ahead. At the front, there was a modest porch in a crumbled state. I suggested to Gopiettan that we go to the porch of the thatched shed for a more comfortable refuge until the rains subsided.

We sprinted our way to the porch and, standing there, watched the rain pour down like crazy. As we stood in a huddle, we noticed a couple of stray dogs also taking shelter on the porch. Just as soaked as we were, their greenish eyes sparkled like emeralds in the darkness. It was an awful sight. We remained still, not wanting to disturb them or risk them pouncing on us. However, reason prevailed, with both parties deciding to coexist peacefully in our rather soggy predicament. With the relentless rain persisting, giving way to restlessness, I casually shifted my gaze to peer inside the thatched house.

The scene inside stuck me with terror; I was stunned to the point of speechlessness. Gopiettan, standing next to me, realized something had gone awry and looked at me quizzically. Unable to express my concerns verbally, I gestured for him to look inside. He did so and instantaneously took a step back to stare at me in utter disbelief, as if struck by a bolt from the blue. Even the pitch-black darkness couldn't conceal the horror etched on his face. Both of us were overcome by a terrible fear that rendered us immobilized. What we saw inside was incredibly horrifying and unnerving: an elderly, bald man clad in red robes, resembling a sorcerer, was seen performing some kind of ritual inside. Around him were a few brass lamps lit up and placed alongside a large, intricate tantrik pattern made from powdered rice and turmeric. With his bulging eyes resembling blazing pieces of charcoal, he looked utterly abominable. The man had smeared holy ash on all visible parts of his body, and beads of sweat had filled his large forehead. Against the backdrop of flickering lamps, he appeared to be performing witchcraft, making incantations to conjure up an evil spirit. Not far from him, I found the severed head of a man kept on a copper platter in a small puddle of blood, and its eyelids were batting. The atmosphere inside was surreal, inducing a nauseating sensation.

Outside, the rain had now considerably abated, and the dogs had vanished by then. The entire area was cloaked in impenetrable darkness. The first thought that came to my mind was to escape from the place, but my legs felt heavy and stuck deeply to the ground, making any movement impossible. As if expressing solidarity with our miserable plight, a bolt of lightning descended from the heavens, sufficiently illuminating the surroundings. In that fleeting flash, I caught sight of the vague outline of a hooded figure standing just next to Gopiettan. Terribly alarmed, I clung to

Gopiettan's hand tightly and literally dragged him out of the porch. Together, we fled the place without pause, only stopping when we reached the safety of the main road. We continued our sprint in the light drizzle, not slowing down until we reached home.

The incident left us with no appetite. However, to maintain a semblance of normality, we settled for a light dinner and went to bed. Fearing a caustic rebuke from my father, we decided to keep the traumatic tale between the two of us. The most formidable challenge before us was finding peaceful sleep that night. My mind churned with thoughts of what we had witnessed in that dreadful place. The sight of the decapitated head placed on a platter with its eyelids fluttering kept flashing in my brain. I also remembered, in the brief instant I glanced into the room, seeing a big cloth bundle drenched in blood lying next to the sorcerer. I closed my eyes tightly, trying to catch some sleep somehow.

The next morning, I woke up feeling slightly feverish. Gopiettan was still sound asleep, seemingly unaffected by the events of the previous night. Despite putting on a facade of normalcy, mother sensed some abnormality on my face. Without yielding to her penetrative looks, I made my way to the front courtyard with a cup of tea in hand, where father was engaged in a conversation with our domestic help, Ravunni. They were seriously discussing planting saplings of plantains around the backyard farm, taking advantage of the ideal soil conditions after the overnight rains.

Sitting on a chair with the cup of tea in hand, I quietly listened to their discussion. After they finished, my father threw a quick glance at me and immediately noticed my distraught look. He had a probing look on his face. Unable to hide the petrifying incident any longer, I wanted to come clean as quickly as possible. After gulping down the remaining tea and setting the cup aside, I narrated the entire incident to my father. There was no immediate reaction on his face, as he wasn't one to easily warm up to fiction or incidents of a similar nature. However, Ravunni's reaction appeared contrasting. He seemed familiar with the place, having heard stories from others that painted it as haunted—a spot shunned even during daylight hours.

Now, it was Ravunni's turn, and he went on to share the information he was privy to. He said he had heard about an enigmatic character who used to visit the place occasionally. This man purportedly had a reputation for possessing mystical abilities and often dabbled in sorcery for those who came seeking his help. Many people approached him with money to harm their adversaries. He had two fierce-looking dogs guarding him, on whom he heavily depended as trusted aides in accomplishing his sinister pursuits. These dogs were extremely loyal, never allowing anyone to even go near the place and protecting their master day and night.

However, one day, someone who had fallen victim to the black magic performed by this sorcerer managed to get past the dogs by poisoning them and enter the house. An intense argument ensued, escalating into a violent altercation. In a fit of rage, the intruder brutally killed the sorcerer with a machete he had carried with him and fled from the place. The murder remained undiscovered until a petty thief, who had ventured into the isolated house in search of something to steal, noticed a body with a severed head lying on the floor. He hastily retreated from the premises, but not before informing a store owner on the main road.

Through some mysterious means, news of the murdered sorcerer reached his guru, possibly through telepathy. In the night, the guru inconspicuously moved the body away from the police, intending to reunite the body and head to resurrect his deceased disciple. For this purpose, the guru visited the location on specified days and performed rituals of black magic.

Taking their time, the police arrived the next morning but were unable to locate the victim's body or the severed head. Despite launching an all-out search operation lasting for two days in the surrounding areas, no clues came to light. However, the police managed to find a breakthrough when they recovered the murder weapon, a machete, from a nearby abandoned well. After piecing together certain other pieces of information, they apprehended the suspect with the help of their dog squad and arrested him. Unfortunately, the police couldn't establish the charge of murder because they failed to retrieve the victim's body. The man who was nabbed by the police continued to languish in jail for several months. No one came forward to seek bail for him, and eventually, he died in his prison cell, bringing the case to a close. Perhaps it was a form of natural retribution that he deserved.

This was one version of the incident that circulated through the grapevine. Perhaps there were a few other stories floating around in the village, but nobody could validate the stories with hard facts or tie up the loose ends to produce a credible account of exactly what had happened in that house on that fateful day. After listening to Ravunni, it struck me that the dogs we confronted on the porch could potentially be the spirits of the same ones that the deceased sorcerer had raised for his protection. However, I was clueless about the identity of the figure in silhouette form standing next to Gopiettan on the porch. Maybe he was the man who was apprehended by the police for murder and later died in prison. Was he waiting outside for an opportunity to ambush the sorcerer and eliminate him for attempting to revive his nemesis? The mysterious ritual the sorcerer was performing with the severed head also baffled me. Was he attempting to bring his disciple back to life? If so, did he succeed in reviving him, and where had they disappeared? Anyway, it was a small gathering of spirits in various forms under the roof of the thatched hut, and it was our good luck that we escaped from them narrowly, avoiding becoming one among them.

Unfortunately, there was no one to provide answers to these questions. The sorcerer and possibly his resurrected disciple might be freely roaming in this small world, continuing their sorcery to harm people for money.

Leaving behind the thoughts, I picked up my tea cup and headed for the dining room. There, I found Goipettan sitting with a cup of tea in front of him and a thermometer thrust in the mouth.

CHAPTER EIGHT

LONGING FOR SALVATION: THE TALE OF AN UNSATIATED SPIRIT

In the bustling city of Calcutta lived my maternal uncle, a prominent figure in his own right. He had four children, and among them was Komal, a pretty-looking woman who had married Gopal, a marine engineer by profession. Their lives took a tragic turn when Gopal suffered a severe injury to his spine while working on a ship in Chennai. The injury was so severe that he needed to be shifted to Calcutta for better medical attention. Gopal's back had borne the brunt of the accident, resulting in a complex fracture that deeply worried the family. Despite their relentless efforts to secure the best available medical care, Gopal's fate hung in the balance, relying on divine intervention and good fortune.

Word reached my uncle about a renowned Ayurvedic herbal oil produced at the Muttikkulangara Vaidysala, situated near Palakkad in Kerala. Filled with hope, he flew down to Kerala to procure this herbal remedy for his son-in-law. Despite the enormous reputation the herbal oil commanded, it failed to produce the expected results. Eventually, Gopal succumbed to his injuries, leaving Komal and the family in extreme grief and gloom.

A few months after the grieving period, Komal, grappling with managing everything alone on the home front, decided to hire a maid to handle their household chores. As time went on, the maid began to experience bizarre occurrences in the house; she claimed to have seen an indistinct figure at various places in the house on numerous occasions. According to her, the hazy figure would appear momentarily and then vanish without a trace. Initially dismissing it as a delusion, she did not consider it serious. However, as the mysterious presence became more frequent, she started feeling increasingly perturbed and concerned.

In the following days, the maid began to see the figure more clearly, confirming that it was a man. However, these incidents failed to convince Komal, who suspected the maid of playing mischief. Nonetheless, she instructed the maid to inform her immediately whenever she noticed the figure in the house. But it never happened because there was no fixed time or place for its appearance. When the figure did manifest, it would disappear hastily. The maid, however, provided a detailed description of the mysterious person she claimed to have repeatedly seen.

To Komal's sheer astonishment, the maid's descriptions perfectly matched every minute detail of Gopal's appearance. The features of the indistinct figure she spoke about bore an uncanny resemblance to those of Gopal, whom the maid had never met in person. This revelation left Komal both perplexed and deeply concerned. She discussed the peculiar occurrences with her father, but he remained sceptical, suspecting that the maid might be insinuating things to deceive them. He believed she could have stumbled upon some old photographs of Gopal in their family album and might be trying to mislead them insidiously with some ulterior motive.

Komal now found herself in a state of anguish, torn between the maid's puzzling sightings and her father's irrational scepticism. Despite her father's suspicions, Komal began to believe that the maid's findings unequivocally suggested the presence of an invisible spirit in the house. This vexing issue persisted for some time until Komal happened to see the mysterious figure herself, turning her life upside down.

On one fateful night, Komal awoke from her sleep to find Gopal sitting at the foot of her bed, gazing at her with a gentle smile. She was shocked and became numb with fear. The shock left her unable to move or cry out for help. In a matter of moments, the apparition rose from the bed and slowly disappeared into the darkness, leaving Komal dazed and deeply shaken.

Early next morning, Komal called her father and narrated this strange incident to him over the phone. He initially sounded extremely concerned and bemused. But, after a few days, he reverted to his sceptical posture and disregarded the occurrence as nothing more than a hallucination caused by her deranged state of mind.

However, the disturbing incidents didn't end there. One day, her father witnessed the spectre of Gopal in his own home. The shadowy figure appeared in the darkness of his bedroom and vanished when he switched on the light. This happened on a regular basis, leaving him in a state of complete uncertainty and chaos.

My father was Komal's father's brother-in-law, and they occasionally remained in touch with each other through letters. After learning about the traumatic events in Komal's life, my father inferred that it was Gopal's spirit seeking to transmit a message by making his presence known in their homes.

My father explained to him that it was not without reason that it was believed that the departed soul often lingered around their loved ones until it attained 'moksha,' or salvation. 'Moksha' offered liberation from the struggles and suffering of the material world, breaking the cycle of life, death, and rebirth. My father strongly believed that the incidents in their homes were indications of the soul's yearning for the proper death rituals to unite the departed soul with the Supreme Being. Maybe the rituals weren't conducted in a proper manner after his death, which could be the reason why Gopal's spirit often visited the place. It served as a reminder for his wife and father-in-law about the importance of performing the rituals properly for his soul to attain salvation. He advised him to come down to Kerala and perform the requisite religious ceremonies, which are quintessential for allowing the departed soul to attain peace and salvation.

Taking my father's advice, he travelled to Kerala and performed all the sacred ceremonies at the Thirunavaya Sree Nava Mukunda temple, located on the beautiful banks of the Bharatapuzha. During his weeklong stay, he also visited numerous temples, fervently seeking solace for the soul and its ultimate attainment of 'moksha'. The ceremonies were performed with the utmost reverence and devotion, and as a result, the fearful sightings in their homes in Calcutta ceased to occur.

The incidents surrounding Gopal's spirit raised more questions than answers about the beliefs and rituals associated with the afterlife. In many cultures and religions, it was believed that after death, a soul lingered around in earthly dominion, seeking peace and salvation. Komal's father, a philosopher himself, sought to arrive at a logical conclusion regarding the theory surrounding the soul and its journey after a person's death. In this regard, he conducted extensive research, closely associating himself with some of the spiritually exalted saints of Calcutta and nearby areas. After concluding his research, he realized that various rituals and ceremonies were essential to help the departed soul peacefully reincarnate into another body. Until then, it wandered aimlessly in the universe around its near and dear ones in pursuit of salvation.

His studies also revealed that before undergoing these rituals, the departed soul remained in a state known as 'preta,' essentially an unsettled and potentially malevolent spirit. After the completion of the ritual, the soul transformed into a 'pitr,' a benevolent spirit, and was harmoniously incorporated into the ancestral lineage. This transition symbolised the soul's evolution from a state of restlessness and detachment to one of tranquilly and unity with the spiritual realm, ancestors, and deities.

His research also led to the exploration of a vast array of theories, revolving around the concept of the soul's journey after death and its persisting attachment to the mortal world. He learned that the purpose of these elaborate rituals was to guide the departed soul to its rightful place among the ancestors and deities. These rituals often involved poojas, prayers, and offerings meant to appease and guide the soul on its journey to the afterlife.

CHAPTER NINE

PILGRIMAGE TO SABARIMALA AND THE MYSTERIOUS MECHANIC

Sabarimala, a renowned Hindu pilgrimage centre dedicated to Lord Ayyappa, possessed several unique features and attracted millions of devotees every year. Swami Ayyappa, the presiding deity of Sabarimala, believed to be celibate and regarded as a composite deity, embodied elements of both Lord Shiva and Lord Vishnu.

Before embarking on their pilgrimage to Sabarimala, devotees were required to maintain vratham (observance) for 41 days. The strict adherence to vows and penance symbolized their enormous commitment to the deity. The pilgrimage, with its challenges and rituals, became a transformative journey for many, fostering spiritual growth and purification. During this period, they were required to lead an ascetic life, faithfully observing religious precepts.

My father had been a dedicated devotee of Lord Ayyappa throughout his life, visiting Sabarimala for many years after faithfully completing the 41-day observance. He had his own group of pilgrims who accompanied him on this spiritual journey.

However, during one season, he had to deviate from his regular group. His eldest brother's son-in-law, whom we called Radhakrishnettan, expressed his wish to undertake the pilgrimage in that season and requested that my father accompany him and his friend Sreekumar on their first visit to the holy shrine of Sabarimala. Radhakrishnettan worked at Cochin Refineries and proposed to make the pilgrimage in his car. As there were only the three of them and the car had ample space, I received an unexpected call to join their group. I was in the eighth standard then, and it was going to be my second visit to the Sabarimala temple. I felt very delighted about the serendipitous opportunity that came my way and grabbed it with both hands.

Perceiving it as an unexpected call from Lord Ayyappa, I began preparations for the pilgrimage in right earnest. However, as the offer came a bit late in the middle of the season, it was not possible for me to undergo the rigours of the mandatory 41-day 'observance' period. Yet, considering it was the wish of Lord Ayyappa for a noble objective, I found myself compelled to make a compromise on principles, presuming that it was acceptable for Lord Ayyappa. The age-old maxim 'the end justifies the means' saved me on that occasion.

After conducting the 'Kettunira' ceremony at my father's elder brother's residence, our pilgrimage began at the crack of dawn on the planned day. The journey in the comfortable and capacious Ambassador car was enjoyable. On the way, we visited various popular temples and made occasional stopovers at hotels to refresh ourselves. These breaks not only offered Radhakrishnettan and his companion a welcome break from the monotony of continuous driving but also ensured that neither of them felt overly fatigued during the day-long ride.

By 3 o'clock in the afternoon, we reached Erumeli, a crucial location along the Sabarimala route. At Erumeli, the huge and sprawling mosque constructed in memory of 'Vavar', a Muslim friend of Lord Ayyappa, was a sight to behold. It was customary for pilgrims to pay their respects at this revered mosque during their pilgrimage to Sabarimala. Unfortunately, our schedule was so tight that time was rapidly slipping away, as we intended to reach 'Pamba,' the base camp for the Sabarimala ascent, by 6:30 in the evening. We still had approximately 88 kilometers left to cover to reach Pamba. Keeping this tight schedule in mind, the elders in the car made the unanimous decision to skip the visit to the mosque at 'Erumeli' and pressed on, determined to reach 'Pamba' as quickly as possible.

As we left Erumeli behind by a fair distance, the car unexpectedly began to huff and puff, showing some serious technical problems. The engine began to sputter, and smoke started billowing out from under the car's hood before it eventually came to a complete stop. The location was a fringe area of Ranni, surrounded by forests with no visible signs of human habitation nearby. Radhakrishnettan was at the wheel, and he swiftly stepped out of the car, followed by Sreekumar uncle. They opened the car's hood, inspecting various crucial electrical points, but couldn't identify any obvious issues. Noticing the dejection on their faces, my father and I also exited the car, hopeful to find some assistance from someone.

Half an hour passed, and as we continued to stand by the roadside, visibly anguished and nonplussed, two neatly dressed Muslim individuals appeared out of nowhere. In their white dhotis and shirts, they seemed to be clerics from a nearby mosque.

Seeing us stranded on the roadside in a distraught state, the clerics approached us and inquired if we needed any assistance. Radhakrishnettan, apparently hesitant due to their appearance, wasn't particularly inclined to accept their help. However, his friend Sreekumar briefed them about the mechanical problem that had left the car immobile. With the car's hood open to cool off the engine and allow the smoke to dissipate, the lead man of the two, wearing a friendly smile, volunteered to have a look inside. After checking the critical components under the hood and finding no issues, he appeared ready to try something different. Removing his white headgear and handing it to his companion, he knelt on the road and slid underneath the car to inspect its undercarriage.

With remarkable dexterity, he toiled hard under the car, trying to fix the glitch. A short while later, he called out for the toolbox, and Radhakrishnettan retrieved one from the car's trunk, pushing it under. The next few minutes resonated with the clanging of spanners and the creaking of nuts. In another five minutes, the man emerged from beneath the car, dusting off his hands, while a euphoric smile lit up his sweaty face. He asked Radhakrishnettan to start the car and drive a short distance to check if everything was working well.

Radhakrishnettan got back into the car, turned the ignition on, and the car started on the first attempt. He then revved up the engine for a while before driving along the road for a few yards and returning. To the amazement of everyone, the car was now running smoothly, with the carburettor showing no signs of overheating, nor was there any trace of smoke emitting from the engine. Radhakrishnettan's initial mistrust in the man's ability to repair cars quickly dissolved, and he expressed his profound gratitude to both the clerics with folded hands. Acknowledging our gratitude with gentle smiles, they continued on their way ahead.

This unexpected brush with strangers not only successfully resolved our car issue but also left an indelible impact, instilling in us a tremendous amount of appreciation for the kindness and chivalry they demonstrated when we were in dire need. It served as a poignant reminder that assistance could come from the most unexpected quarters, and it would be foolish to judge someone solely based on appearance. This incident served as an eye-opener for us, underscoring the universal truth that human kindness knows no bounds.

As the clerics departed, an astonishing sight caught our attention. The white shirt and dhoti of the man who had crawled under the dusty and grimy undercarriage of the car appeared as impeccably clean and immaculate as they were when he first approached us. There wasn't a speck of dirt or soil adhering to his sparkling white attire. It was something so unusual that we found it hard to believe. Just as we watched them leave in utter disbelief, the two men veered into the dense forest and swiftly disappeared into the lush foliage.

With the memory of the unexpected meeting with those strangers still playing in our minds, we continued our journey to 'Pamba.' During the drive, my father, with the richness of age and experience behind him, suggested that it might have been a gentle admonition from Lord Ayyappa, disapproving of our decision not to visit the mosque at 'Erumeli.' He believed that the men, appearing in the attire of clerics, were deputed by none other than 'Vavar' himself, acting upon the will of Lord Ayyappa, to extend their helping hand to us. I found some merit in his version of the incident, and the belief took firm root in my heart, considering the remote and secluded nature of the surroundings from where they sprang up. The landscape passed through a dense forest, devoid of any signs of human habitation, and the unexpected appearance of those two men offering unsolicited assistance to repair the car seemed nothing short of a miraculous intervention.

In due course, we reached 'Pamba,' the holy base camp, and promptly began our ascent towards the sacred shrine of Lord Ayyappa atop the mountain. After experiencing a spiritually gratifying darshan of the Lord, we commenced our descent early the next morning. The drive from Pampa, cutting through the misty morning weather, was exhilarating. On our way back, Radhakrishnettan intentionally made a stop at a roadside tea stall in Ranni, a little away from the place where we had been stranded during our onward journey.

As the teashop was bustling with Ayyappa devotees, we chose to stand outside and enjoy our tea. The tea stall owner, dressed in a black dhoti and visibly an Ayyappa devotee himself, stepped out of his cash counter and casually engaged us in a conversation about topics ranging from the current rush to the facilities provided at the temple. Seizing this opportunity, Radhakrishnettan broached the topic of the strange incident that had occurred the previous evening when our car had experienced a mechanical issue while passing through this very location and how two Muslim clerics had appeared out of nowhere and fixed the problem.

As Radhakrishnettan narrated the story, the tea stall owner listened intently and showed no sign of surprise. Confirming the occurrence of many such incidents that had happened from time to time, he mentioned that pilgrims who chose to skip visiting the mosque at 'Erumeli' often faced these strange situations. According to the tea stall owner, the man dressed in white cleric attire who fixed the problem with our car was none other than 'Vavar' himself, not someone deputed by him, as inferred by my father.

Within half an hour, we reached 'Erumeli.' Radhakrishnettan parked the car in a designated parking area, and all of us disembarked. We then proceeded to the expansive white-marbled mosque dedicated to 'Vavar,' seeking forgiveness for not visiting this sacred place the previous day. We took the opportunity to express our deepest gratitude to 'Vavar' for his timely assistance in resolving the difficult situation we had faced at Ranni. The incident served as a pointer towards the excellent relationship between Lord Ayyappa and 'Vavar,' emphasising the belief that, for Lord Ayyappa, the mosque held as much importance as his own divine abode at Sabarimala. As we departed from 'Erumeli,' an overwhelming feeling of contentment washed over us.

As the years passed, my mindset underwent a transformation, leading me to harbour doubts about the narratives portraying 'Vavar' as Lord Ayyappa's friend. In childhood, innocence and gullibility defined my perspective, and I lacked the wisdom to sift through the heaps of fallacies and fiction that had been passed down through generations. Consequently, the interpretations provided by the elders regarding the incident at Ranni became deeply ingrained in my psyche.

It was only as I matured and gained wisdom that my perceptions of the supposed mysterious incident at Ranni, which occurred many years ago, inevitably evolved. During this period, I encountered numerous authentic stories of Ayyappa that shed more light on his life. From these writings, I discovered that Ayyappan had a bodyguard named 'Vapuran,' who commanded the area around Erumeli. It occurred to me that his name might have been altered to 'Vavar' by some revisionist historians aiming to infuse a touch of secularism into the tales of Lord Ayyappa.

What perplexed me the most was the realization that Lord Ayyappa existed prior to the emergence of Islam. Therefore, it defied all logic to believe that he had an Islamic friend before the advent of that religion.

CHAPTER TEN

WHISPERS IN THE DARK: STORY OF A HAUNTED APARTMENT

During my bachelor days in Bombay, I lived with my four friends in the CGS Quarters located at Antop Hill, a downtown area just east of the Harbour railway station, Guru Teg Bahadur Nagar, formerly known as Koliwada. It was a massive colony of residential quarters constructed for Central Government employees. Interestingly, only a few of the allottees stayed in the colony, while the others rented out their flats to outsiders in order to supplement their income. Though this practice was against the rules, it thrived, providing affordable housing options for bachelors like us and many others. The tenancy agreements for these rented flats ran for a duration of eleven months, and as our agreement was nearing its end, we were actively searching for a new flat, preferably in the same building or nearby.

One evening, while dining at the popular Hotel Janith in Koliwada, the hotel manager, Thomas, introduced us to Ashok, a broker who acted as a middleman between the allottees of the quarters and prospective tenants. Ashok informed us that he had a good three-bedroom apartment in his custody in Sector 7 for immediate occupancy for a rent lower than the prevailing market rates. For us, it was a handsome deal worth considering.

The next day, Ashok took us to visit the three-bedroom apartment. It was indeed good, but what piqued our interest was the low rent quoted for it. Ashok explained that three-bedroom apartments were not in high demand in the rental market, as smaller flats were consistently sought after. Typically, larger flats attracted higher rent, and tenants, who mostly belonged to the middle-class section, could not afford such accommodations. For us, the only downside was that the flat was on the top floor, which could make the heat unbearable during scorching summer months due to the heat radiating down from the terrace.

Soon, money changed hands, and we took possession of the flat within a week. Everything was facilitated through Ashok, and we never had the opportunity to meet the allottee even once, nor did we show any inclination to meet him. However, Ashok had referred to the allottee's name during one of the negotiating rounds, but none of us could recall it just a few days later.

On the first Sunday after receiving the keys, we shifted to the flat. Only a handful of occupants resided in the building, and there was no one on the fourth floor as a neighbour for us. The building consisted of three wings, each leading to a common terrace. From the terrace, one could enjoy a panoramic view of the entire Antop Hill and its neighbouring areas, such as Matunga and Dadar. The apartment's three bedrooms imparted a spacious feel, and since we were only five members, we decided to use only two of them to have a check on electricity consumption. The third room served as a place for keeping our belongings and also for hanging our used clothes. A couple of clotheslines were tied across the room using the window grills for the clothes to hang nicely. For sleeping purposes, Jayaprakash and I occupied one room, while the others—Prakash, Ajith, and Preman—shared the other. I had known Jayaprakash from my college days, and he had come to Bombay with the purpose of relocating to Dubai in pursuit of a promising job opportunity.

The days began smoothly in the new house. Within a matter of days, we developed a cordial relationship with a man named Mishra, who ironed clothes near the staircase on the ground floor. Mishra assured us that he would take care of all our ironing needs and would be available seven days a week, from morning until evening. Interestingly, his ironing table also served as a cot for the night-duty watchman, who consistently appeared in the evenings in an inebriated state. Nevertheless, he played the role of 'man Friday' for most residents, assisting them in procuring essentials from nearby shops in the mornings. Perhaps the watchman found the ironing board below the staircase more inviting for a restful night's sleep than his own home and the company of his family.

On a weekend, two of our friends, Ravi and his younger brother Haridas, dropped by our place for an overnight stay. Rummy had been our favourite passion when all of us gathered, and on that day, too, we sat down to play the game till beyond midnight. When it was time to retire for the night, Jayaprakash and I offered our bedroom to our guests, choosing to make ourselves comfortable in the smaller bedroom used for keeping our belongings. The bedroom had a petite cot, and since Jayaprakash's height exceeded six feet, he wouldn't fit on it. So, I slept on the cot while Jayaprakash settled on a plastic mat on the floor.

A few minutes into my sleep, I was abruptly jolted awake by a violent gasp, as if an invisible force were attempting to suffocate me. I struggled vigorously to free myself from the grip around my neck. Beads of chilled perspiration clung to my forehead, breathlessness constricting me, and my heart pounded like a jackhammer. In my panicked attempts to break free, I let out a shriek that cut through the silence, startling Jayaprakash and rousing him from his sleep.

Still grappling with a sensation of suffocation, I told Jayaprakash what I had experienced in my sleep. It felt as if someone had tried to strangle me by pressing a pillow forcefully onto my face. Jayaprakash tried to pacify me, suggesting that it might have been a nightmare, and asked me to go back to sleep. He brought me a glass of water; after gulping it down, I went to sleep once again.

The following morning, we casually referred the incident to Prakash, but he simply shrugged it off with his trademark smirk. He was sure that it must have been a bad dream or the aftereffects of the previous night's extended gaming session. Our guests departed the next evening, and Jayaprakash and I resumed sleeping in our usual bedroom. Nothing untoward or extraordinary happened thereafter.

A few days later, Jayaprakash and I arrived home late at night after dining out. We were getting ready for bed, while the others had already retired to their room. As we turned off all the lights and headed to our room, faint groans reached our ears from the small bedroom. Walking up to the door, we listened to the peculiar sounds. The groans continued, accompanied by the sound of heavy breathing. Curious, we opened the door to see who was inside, and the squeaking sound of the door handle abruptly silenced the noise.

We entered the room and turned on the light. To our surprise, there was no one inside. It appeared that someone had struggled on the small cot, given the appearance of the crumpled bedsheet and pillows. We called out to the others from their room and told them about the bizarre incident. They all hurried to the small bedroom but found nothing inside except for the dishevelled bed and crumpled pillows. Prakash, as was his habit, ruled that one of us, who had entered that bedroom the previous night to hang their used clothes, might have accidentally left the bedsheet and pillows in a disorganized state. While this explanation seemed plausible, the mysterious groaning and panting sounds left us puzzled, making it difficult to arrive at a conclusive answer. The resolution to this mystery finally came to the fore a few days later.

It was when I arrived home from the office a bit earlier than usual. As I headed to the small bedroom to change my clothes and hang the used ones on the rope, I was surprised to find our clothes scattered all over the floor, despite having been neatly hung on the rope. Moreover, the bedsheet on the cot was once again in disarray, giving the impression that someone had entered the room and engaged in a struggle on the bed during our absence.

Initially, I suspected that it might have been an attempted burglary by thieves. However, there was no conceivable way that the thieves could have gained access to our securely locked apartment without breaking the lock. To add to the mystery, nothing had gone missing either. When Jayaprakash came home, I showed him the room, and together we attempted to join the dots and piece together a coherent picture, linking it to the previous incident, but it led us nowhere.

Another two weeks passed without any unusual incidents. Then, one night, Jayaprakash abruptly woke me from my sleep and urged me to listen to the strange sounds coming from the small bedroom. We both rose from our beds, our ears finely tuned to the mysterious noises emerging from the room. The initial muffled groans soon escalated into plaintive wails with occasional sounds of footsteps, as if someone were moving inside very slowly, with the footwear dragging along the floor.

We woke our friends in their bedroom and told them in hushed voices about the sounds coming from the small bedroom. It seemed unbelievable to them at first. Rubbing the sleep away, all of them joined us at the door of the small bedroom. As we stood, listening intently, the sounds gradually faced away. Once the situation had completely stabilized, we opened the door very carefully and turned on the light. There was nobody inside, yet we once again discovered signs of a struggle: clothes that had been hanging on the lines were now strewn around in a heap on the floor, and the bedsheet was in a crumpled state beneath the bed. This was enough to convince the others that something truly unusual was occurring in that small bedroom.

This peculiar series of events persisted almost every night. It became the new normal for us, and it was starting to affect us badly. Following these inexplicable events, we shifted all our belongings from the small bedroom to other rooms and started sleeping together in one room. We kept the small room locked permanently, and none of us dared to go near it, even during daylight hours. A palpable trepidation had gripped all of us to the extent that those returning home early from work in the evenings intentionally delayed entering the house. Each one of us chose to hang around near the building until another friend returned from work. Fortunately, we experienced no disturbances during the daytime, and we spent our Sundays and other holidays peacefully at home.

Meanwhile, we seriously considered vacating this flat and relocating to another one as soon as possible. Unfortunately, none of us had Ashok's address or contact number, and he seemed to have disappeared from the circuit. With no other options available to reconnect with Ashok, we thought Hotel Janith was the most likely place where we might run into him once again.

At Hotel Janith, the manager, Thomas, provided us with some grossly disheartening news about the sudden disappearance of Ashok from the scene. He informed us that Ashok had returned to his hometown, presumably facing significant trouble over charges of several money embezzlement issues, and it was highly unlikely that he would return to Antop Hill anytime soon.

As we left the hotel, in a dejected frame of mind, a young man arrived there. He was Basheer, a well-known agent in the area, and Thomas casually introduced him to us. In the absence of Ashok, we thought that Basheer might be able to assist us in finding another flat for rent in quick time. After exchanging greetings with Basheer, we left the place. Before departing, we told him that we were urgently in search of a new flat. However, we felt it was neither the right time nor the appropriate place to discuss the exigency of our requirement with a new acquaintance whom we hardly knew.

A couple of days later, we accidentally ran into Basheer in Sector 7, and he immediately recognized us. This was the opportunity we had been waiting for. As he accompanied us to our building, we casually inquired if he had any information about the whereabouts of Ashok. Basheer felt Ashok was possibly in his hometown, Satara, and might not return soon. However, he assured us that he could help in finding another good apartment at the earliest. By then, we had reached the teashop near our building.

We thought a cup of tea would act as a catalyst for establishing a warm relationship with Basheer, so we stopped by the teashop. We badly needed his assistance in finding an alternative place so that we could move out of the jinxed house as soon as possible. After placing our order, we waited outside for the boy to serve us tea. As a prelude to striking up a conversation, we casually pointed out our building to Basheer, which was right across the road from the teashop. Turning around to have a look, he appeared visibly taken aback as he gazed at the building. Concealing his surprise, he asked if we had experienced any problems during our stay in the flat. Before we could respond, he mentioned that, in general, the building had a reputation for being doomed, particularly a flat on the fourth floor. That's when we disclosed that we were staying in that very flat, and he stared at us in utter disbelief.

The tea arrived, and as we took small sips of the hot brew, we provided a brief account of the unpleasant experiences we had been facing in that flat. After finishing his cup of tea, Basheer lit a cigarette. Exhaling a thick puff of smoke, he told us that he had heard from local residents and his contacts in the police about a tragedy that had occurred in the flat with its previous tenants a few years ago. The allottee of the flat had rented it out to someone, and after this incident came to light, his allotment was cancelled. The flat was then re-allotted to another officer, who continued with the prevailing practice, and that was how we obtained tenancy for that flat. The new allottee kept a low profile and rented out his apartment through agents, never coming into direct contact with his tenants.

Basheer took out another cigarette and lit it. Darkness had covered the surroundings, and as he took a heavy puff, we could see his face illuminated by the fire at the tip of the lit cigarette. Clearing his throat, he began to recount the mysterious incident that had occurred in the flat a few years ago.

A few years ago, a family of three lived on rent in that house. The husband, whose name Basheer couldn't recall, worked for a public limited company, and his wife was a homemaker. They had a young child who attended kindergarten. We knew the husband's name was Gaurav Saxena from the partly broken nameplate that still precariously hung on the main door. Gaurav's wife was Meenakshi, something that we stumbled upon from numerous letters found in the house, apparently from her parents. These letters were discovered during our cleaning operation of the flat.

Once, during the Diwali holidays, Meenakshi and the little kid went to their hometown in Patna to spend vacation, while Gaurav couldn't accompany them due to work pressure in the office. However, he assured her that he would reach Patna one day before Diwali, and they would all return together.

Flicking away the half smoked cigarette, Basheer continued. A few days later, the newspaper boy began noticing something unusual. The newspapers that he delivered each morning continued to remain outside the door. As he came very early in the morning, there was a strict instruction for him not to ring the bell when he dropped off the newspaper. However, the next day, he rang the bell several times, but there was no answer. Sensing something was amiss, he tried inquiring with the watchman, who was leaving for home after a good night's sleep. The dipsomaniac guy that he was had no clue and left the place as if he had better things to do once he got home. As Mishra, the colony's presser, came to his work a little late, the newspaper boy couldn't hang around until then. He went about his regular task of delivering newspapers to others in the colony, but in any case, he discontinued delivering newspapers to that house the next day.

The colony, characterized by its floating population, rarely fostered lasting friendships or connections. Tenants came and went, and rarely did anyone forge bonds with their neighbours. Nobody knew anything about the family who had resided in that flat, where they had come from, or where they had gone. Consequently, the mystery remained unsolved for many days.

When Gaurav didn't arrive as expected, it set off alarm bells for the family in Patna. Their flat in the CGS colony did not have a telephone connection, making it impossible for the family to contact him. As their concern grew, they attempted to reach him through his office's board number. Since it was vacation time, their calls went unanswered. With no other option available to establish contact with Gaurav, Meenakshi made up her mind to return to Bombay immediately. Unfortunately, due to the Diwali rush, there were no tickets available for train or air travel.

Not wanting to send Meenakshi alone with the little child, her father decided to accompany them to Bombay. Two days later, they managed to secure train tickets through an agent. Arriving at Dadar, they hired a taxi to take them to Antop Hill. Mishra, as usual, was engaged in ironing clothes near the staircase, and Meenakshi, without even looking at him, went up the stairs like a whirlwind, with others struggling to catch up with her. What she found on the door to their flat shattered her heart, and she began weeping uncontrollably. A yellow ribbon with bold black letters reading 'POLICE, DO NOT CROSS THE LINE' was tied across it. The lock was also covered with a piece of cloth, with a dab of lac holding its joints together.

Just as we were pondering how Basheer could gather even the minutest of information, he seemed to perceive what was going on in our minds. Bringing a smile on his grim face, he told us that he had been a police informer until a few years ago and still maintained close acquaintances with several officers at the Matunga police station. One of them was part of the investigation team that handled the case, and he used to provide frequent updates on every development to Basheer.

The sound of the azan echoed through a loudspeaker from a nearby mosque. Basheer took a brief pause, allowing the call to prayer to complete. Then he continued from where he had left off. As the commotion drew the attention of the residents, many of them gathered at the entrance of the building. A few elderly men among them prevented others from going up. In a short while, a devastated Meenakshi, followed by her father and daughter, came down weeping all the way.

Mishra, who had paused his ironing job by then, approached Meenakshi's father, and just as he was preparing to say something, a police jeep came screeching to a halt in front of the building. A handful of uniformed policemen and a lady constable got down from it, and after identifying Meenakshi, they asked her to accompany them to the station. Shooing away onlookers, the lady constable led Meenakshi and her family to the waiting jeep. With them, the jeep sped away, leaving a cloud of dust in its wake.

Fearing the worst, Meenakshi kept pleading with the police to disclose what had happened to Gaurav. Despite her desperate appeals, the officers maintained a stony silence. Observing the grim attitude of the police, her father sensed that something dreadful awaited them at the police station. His worst fears were confirmed upon their arrival.

They were guided to a senior police officer, who courteously invited them to take a seat and promptly arranged for water and tea. Thereafter, with a sombre demeanour, the officer conveyed the distressing news: Gaurav had passed away. According to the post-mortem report, the cause of death was considered to be asphyxiation. There was no evidence of a break-in, leaving the police clueless about the circumstances leading to the tragedy. The investigation was proceeding speedily, with the police seriously examining all potential angles to uncover the truth.

All hell broke loose, and taken over by uncontrollable grief, Meenakshi instantly collapsed in the chair. Witnessing the distressing condition of her mother, her little daughter also began to cry. When attempts to pacify Meenakshi proved futile, the police officer asked a female officer to take her and the child to another room and console them. He then calmly explained the sequence of events to her father.

After Meenakshi left for Patna, the woman appointed by the residents' association for the regular collection of kitchen waste became erratic in her visits to the fourth floor, showing up only once or twice a week. Perhaps her past experiences had led her to believe that, in the absence of a lady in the house, there would be minimal waste generated, reducing the need for regular pick-ups. When she finally visited one day, she detected a foul smell emanating from the flat. Alarmed, she rushed downstairs and notified a resident living below, who then alerted the Matunga police station. In response, a team of officers immediately rushed to the building.

The police, accompanied by their sniffer dog, arrived at the scene. They continuously rang the bell and banged on the doors with force. When these efforts did not evoke any response from inside, they broke open the door with the help of a locksmith. Upon entering the flat, they were greeted by an oppressive smell permeating the rooms. In one of the rooms, they discovered a body lying on a cot, already in a state of decay. The dog meticulously explored the entire apartment, sniffing around every nook and cranny before finally returning to the bedroom where the corpse lay. Standing by the side of the window on its hind legs, it started barking vigorously, continuously staring outside through the window. Its eyes were fixated on the endless, overcast sky outside, and oddly enough, there was nothing to be seen except for the vast expanse of grey clouds. Moments later, the dog abruptly turned around, making some unusual sounds, and hastily retreated from the room. It sought refuge behind its handler, clearly displaying signs of alarm or angst.

The police conducted a comprehensive search of the house and took custody of various articles. By midnight, they had completed their procedures and shifted the corpse to the mortuary at J.J. Hospital in an ambulance for embalming and preservation. Simultaneously, the police requested assistance from the officers of the forensic department in Hyderabad, hoping to gain a breakthrough in the investigations. Meanwhile, the police awaited someone from Gaurav's family to claim responsibility for the mortal remains.

The incident received widespread coverage in the local Marathi dailies and English tabloids. The police department's medical team and officers from the Hyderabad Forensic Lab conducted detailed investigations into Gaurav's death. The postmortem report revealed that he died from asphyxiation due to strangulation, leaving the police totally flummoxed. Although it was clear that someone had smothered Gaurav to death, there was no corroborative evidence to support this theory. The flat showed no signs of intrusion, and even the police dog seemed utterly befuddled, running inside the house without a clear direction. Fingerprint experts also failed to provide any conclusive evidence, finding only Gaurav's recent fingerprints throughout the flat with no trace of a second person.

Another factor that baffled the police was why Gaurav's body was found in the small bedroom when he normally slept in the master bedroom. The police were equally stumped by another factor: why there were signs of a struggle in the bedroom where Gaurav was found smothered, especially when there were no indications of forced entry into the flat. Despite their best efforts, the police couldn't make any headway, eventually relegating the case to the backburner. On official records, the case was open and under probe, but it safely remained within the confines of the category of unsolved cases.

With a long sigh, Basheer concluded his story and left the place, bidding farewell to us. We waited until he turned the corner and disappeared from our sight before heading home. It was very late at night, and the tale had left us feeling more frightened. Reaching home, the first thing we did was remove and discard the ill-omened hanging nameplate of Gaurav from the main door. During dinner, we reaffirmed our resolve to leave the CGS colony and relocate to a faraway place from Antop Hill as quickly as possible since nobody wanted to live in that wretched place any longer.

Very soon, Ajith, using his good connections, managed to find a flat in Vashi, a beautiful city across the Thane Creek. We were confident that the spirits of Gaurav or his mysterious killer would not follow us that far.

In hindsight, I held a firm belief that the spirit or soul of an individual who met a tragic or unnatural death remained in the world until the performance of specific rituals that facilitated their journey towards salvation. This belief was deeply ingrained in my consciousness, nurtured, and cultivated through my upbringing. I firmly advocated the significance of conducting the appropriate rituals and ceremonies to assist the departed soul in attaining tranquillity and progressing to the afterlife.

However, a nagging question weighed heavily on my mind, leading me to wonder if the suffocation and struggle I had endured during one of our initial days in that flat had been orchestrated by the same spirit that took the life of Gaurav Saxena. Or, was it the spirit of Gaurav expressing his anger towards the person choosing to sleep on the bed on which he had met his end?

One thing was certain that the original spirit frequenting the place was the one responsible for smothering Gaurav to death, likely provoked by his use of the cot. This implied that the cot in the bedroom had played a shady role in this inexplicable occurrence, forcing all the previous tenants to leave it behind when they vacated the flat. It was conceivable that they, too, faced similar incidents during their stay and narrowly escaped being strangled.

In my case, I might have annoyed the spirit by unwittingly sleeping on that cot. Fortunately, I managed to wriggle out of the grim fate of becoming another wandering spirit, thanks to Jayaprakash, who shared the room with me and slept on a mat. My frantic screams woke him, compelling the vindictive spirit to release its grip on my neck and make a hasty retreat. Unfortunately, Gaurav slept alone on the same cot and had to pay the price with his life.

However, what puzzled me the most was the sound of struggle that frequently originated from the bedroom at midnight. Were the two spirits engaging in a skirmish to outsmart each other or trying to assert their supremacy?

Some mysteries in the universe defy explanation, and it would be unwise to relentlessly pursue answers to such unfathomable questions.

CHAPTER ELEVEN

SHADOWS OF ETERNITY: A NIGHT IN THIRUVATTUR

A year after our wedding in 1987, my wife Suma and I visited our hometown in Kerala, staying at my parental house for nearly a month. During our stay, we took the opportunity to visit several close relatives to introduce the newest member of our family to them, as some of these relatives were unable to attend our wedding in Bombay.

Towards the end of our month-long trip, we paid a visit to one of my elderly paternal aunts, who held high respect within our family. She resided in the sleepy village of Kannapuram in Kannur District, approximately 15 kilometers away from the city. We arrived at her place around noon, with the plan to return in the evening. She was delighted to see Suma, and expressed her profound gratitude to me for bringing her home to seek blessings.

After lunch, as we were engrossed in conversation, my aunt shared a captivating tale about an ancient Shiva temple in Thiruvattur, near Thaliparamba in Kannur. It seemed that the temple held special significance for newlyweds, as its principal deities were Lord Shiva and his consort Parvati. According to local belief, these divine figures possessed the power to bestow blessings upon newlywed couples, granting them peace and prosperity in their conjugal life. She suggested that we visit the temple before returning home, believing it would bring good fortune to our future lives.

Intrigued by her suggestion, I found myself drawn to her wise counsel, despite lacking any prior knowledge of the temple she mentioned or its location. With our return journey to Bombay just a few days away, time became a major constraint, and we had a number of plans lined up for the upcoming days. It was crucial to use the remaining days of our stay judiciously to avoid overrunning our itinerary and missing visits to other scheduled places. However, dismissing my aunt's suggestion outright seemed impolite, particularly given the wisdom often associated with age.

Realizing that making the temple visit that very evening was impossible, she suggested that we spend the night at her place and visit the temple the following day. Fortunately, Suma had the habit of carrying extra clothes, even during short daylong visits, so staying overnight posed no problem.

In the evening, my aunt called home her neighbour, Dasan, who operated an autorickshaw in the village. She requested him to drive us to Thaliparamba the next day, where we could catch a bus to the Thiruvattur temple. Dasan agreed, but there was a problem: he had a prior booking for his auto in the morning, which he couldn't cancel. Nonetheless, he suggested that the afternoon timings would be more suitable for us to have a satisfying darshan at the temple. The temple opened at 6 and closed at 7:30 in the morning, making it a bit inconvenient for us to reach the place during those early hours. Conversely, in the evening, the temple remained open between 5 PM and 7:30 PM, providing ample time to reach there and have darshan. After darshan, we could catch a bus to Thaliparamba and then proceed to the Kannur railway station, from where we could board a train to Kuttippuram, our home station. So, the plan was set accordingly.

It was a time when mobile phones were not as prevalent, and it put paid to my hopes of communicating the change in our plans to my parents back home. My aunt did not have a telephone at her residence either, which meant that the altered travel plans were destined to remain a surprise to my parents back home.

The next day, at 3:30 in the afternoon, Dasan arrived with his autorickshaw to pick us up. We were ready to depart by then, and after bidding farewell to my aunt, we boarded the autorickshaw to leave for Thaliparamba. As the rickshaw moved out of the compound, I turned around a few times to catch a final glimpse of my aunt waving at us from the gate. It was a thoughtful gesture of hers that we were going to have the privilege of visiting a temple highly revered by the people of Kannur and its surrounding areas.

The distance from Kannapuram to Thaliparamba was approximately 14 kilometres, and the entire road was rough and uneven, making the journey quite unpleasant as we swayed and swivelled in his rickshaw along the way. To lighten our ordeal, Dasan engaged us in conversation, narrating fascinating legends about the Thiruvattur temple. Local inhabitants believed that the temple had ancient origins, and the 'shivling' in the sacred inner shrine was considered self-manifested. It possessed immense power, and everyone in the village firmly believed that Lord Shiva resided there in His fierce form, known as 'ugra moorthy.'

Finally, the arduous ride came to an end, and we reached Thaliparamba at approximately 4:30 p.m. Our plan was to hire another rickshaw from there to take us to the Thiruvattoor temple. However, none of the auto drivers were willing to undertake the 22-kilometer journey to Thiruvattoor. The road, it seemed, was marred by potholes and deemed unsuitable for small vehicles. Also, they were concerned about the risk of returning empty, knowing they wouldn't find any passengers for their trip back to Thaliparamba. My tactful attempts to lure them with some extra money were met with stiff resistance, and they remained firm in their resolve, refusing to budge from their stand. They appeared well-acquainted with such offers throughout their lives and, as a result, were wary of taking the bait.

The auto drivers, however, were kind-hearted to propose an alternative solution. They informed us that there was a private bus service that operated between Thaliparamba and Thiruvattoor, and we could take the same to reach the temple. The last trip from Thaliparamba was at about 5 in the evening. This option appeared ideal and we thought to adhere to it. They showed us the direction to the bus station, which was just a short distance away.

With ease, we located the bus station and boarded the bus headed for Thiruvattoor. The bus was almost empty when we stepped on board. Around fifteen minutes later, a few more passengers joined us, and precisely at 5 o'clock, the bus embarked on its journey towards Thiruvattoor. When purchasing our tickets, I requested the conductor to notify us when the bus reached our destination.

The bus ride was no different, and after 45 minutes of a bumpy journey, we arrived at what seemed to be the quaint hamlet of Thiruvattoor. The conductor's loud announcement from the rear of the bus confirmed that we had reached our destination. Quickly, we got off from the bus and took a moment to absorb our surroundings as the bus continued on its way, kicking up plumes of dust and making an irritating noise that disrupted the serenity of the place. The location appeared authentic and unspoiled, seamlessly blending into the backdrop of a hill and thick vegetation.

Next to the bus stop on the left, we found a small shop and a reading room, both of which were closed at that hour. On the right side of the road stood what seemed to be a primordial banyan tree, silently bearing witness to the temple's ancient existence. A narrow pathway extended from this venerable tree towards the temple, situated about a hundred meters away. Without delay, we strolled gently towards our sacred destination.

As we approached the temple, a prehistoric stone pathway flanked by tall trees on either side, witnesses to generations of devotees seeking solace and divine blessings, beckoned us forward. The temple's architecture was a testament to its glorious past, showcasing intricate carvings on weathered stone walls that narrated stories of gods, goddesses, mythical beings, and significant events from ancient epics. Its design flawlessly fused traditional craftsmanship with timeless artistry, eliciting wonder and admiration among the devotees who came to visit.

The temple's surroundings oozed a tranquil ambiance, enhancing the spiritual experience for those undertaking this pilgrimage. Within the temple compound, a spacious courtyard served as what appeared to be a gathering place for religious ceremonies, festivals, and community events. Its two-tiered sanctum sanctorum had a rectangular shape, topped with copper sheets on the roof. A towering flag mast stood proudly in front of it, coated with brass, adding to the temple's majestic presence. Also standing right in front of the sanctum sanctorum was a tall, multi-tiered circular lamp crafted from granite stone. It featured numerous small, recessed spaces designed for pouring oil and placing wicks to illuminate them.

Only a couple of individuals were present at the temple, their inquisitive gazes clearly indicating their unfamiliarity with our faces in their village or the nearby areas. Acknowledging their quizzical glances with a gentle bow, we proceeded to enter the inner shrine. There was absolute silence all around. The diminutive wooden door at the main passage leading to the inner shrine, which housed the primary deity, had a weathered, ageing flower garland hung on it. The dark, slimy oil lamps on either side displayed wicks charred to the halfway point, devoid of any residual oil, indicating sporadic usage. Perhaps they were lit up only on special occasions; nonetheless, a solitary lamp remained aglow, its flickering flame dispensing radiance as a symbolic offering to keep the deity within in good humour.

Inside, the small door leading to the inner sanctum was shut, and we could hear the recitation of mantras and the sound of a bell ringing. Patiently, we stood before the closed doors, hands folded, awaiting the moment when the priest would open them, granting us a glimpse of the all-powerful and mighty deity residing within. Finally, the doors swung open one by one, granting us a glimpse of the all-powerful and mighty deity in its full glory and the experience was truly mesmerizing. It unveiled the 'shivling' in its ethereal form and magnificent glory. The lamp placed in front of it emitted a myriad of lustrous reflections through a skillfully arranged mirror crafted from pieces of glass behind the 'shivling', bathing it in a serene and divine beauty.

We remained there in contemplative prayer for a few more seconds, completely absorbed in the divine atmosphere. Afterwards, we proceeded to offer our respects to the idol of Parvathy, the beloved consort of Lord Shiva. While the priest was drawing water from a small well within the temple's inner sanctum, we approached him with a request to perform a few offerings to the Lord in our names. He noted our names and birth stars before re-entering the inner shrine.

A few minutes later, the priest came out and handed us some flowers and sweet-smelling sandalwood paste, all neatly tucked in a fresh banana leaf. After offering him a dakshina, which essentially represented a token of gratitude and respect given to a priest for their guidance, services, and blessings, we made our exit from the inner shrine.

As we stepped outside, the two men waiting near the temple approached us, intent on striking up a conversation to satisfy their curiosity. One of them was the oracle of the temple, a deduction I made from his long hair and traces of turmeric found in the parting of his hair. He walked with a noticeable limp, evidently affected by a painful corn on the sole of his foot, and I recalled that many of the oracles I knew had similar issues to contend with. They warmly inquired about the place where we came from, as our faces were unfamiliar to them and they hadn't seen us in their village before. While I gave them satisfactory answers to all their questions, the priest also joined our conversation after locking the inner shrine and the main temple doors. It was evident that all of them were preparing to leave the temple for their homes. Just as they were about to leave, I enquired if we could find an autorickshaw there to go to Thaliparamba so that we could catch a train to Kannur from there.

My words brought them to a sudden stop. They turned around, and the oracle tersely conveyed that finding an autorickshaw from Thiruvattur to Thaliparamba would be impossible. Even during the daytime, rickshaws were reluctant to travel to this location. As he spoke, the unmistakable consternation on each of their faces hinted at the hardships awaiting us that night in Thiruvattur. However, he offered a suggestion: we could try our luck by catching the same bus that had brought us there. This bus was scheduled to make its final trip to Thaliparamba, passing through Thiruvattur around 7:30 p.m. It was nearly 7 o'clock, so we still had time. However, the suggestion came with the forewarning from the priest that the bus occasionally cancelled its last trip due to a lack of passenger patronage. The odds were heavily stacked against us, but we decided to take our chances, placing our faith in the benevolence of Lord Shiva to guide us through this challenging situation, as we had no other alternatives to fall back on.

While they left for their homes, taking a road behind the temple, we went down to the bus stop opposite the giant banyan tree. We waited at the bus stop for an hour or so, but there was no sign of the bus. Anxiety started to creep in, especially because I wasn't alone; I had to take care of Suma too. Hunger and thirst were the other two elements I had to deal with. Luckily, Suma had a bottle of water to quench my thirst, but unfortunately, there were no means to address the hunger, and it was left to remain unattended.

Another half-hour passed, and the entire place was plunged into darkness. The continuous sound of rustling of the banyan tree leaves in the gentle breeze sowed seeds of concern in our minds. As the night wore on and thin layers of mist gradually descended, we felt it was not sensible to stand under the roofless bus stop for any longer. The reading room, a modest structure made of dried palmyra leaves adjacent to the bus stop, appeared to be a safe option to seek refuge under. Much to our relief, we found two slightly weathered benches there, placed on the front porch. Across the road, a streetlight pole under the massive banyan tree offered a faint glimmer of light, but beyond that, darkness held its reign. Amidst this darkness and mist, I could discern the outlines of the range of hills that encircled the area from all sides. The faint, trickling sounds of water streaming down the nearby river were the only sounds that disrupted the prevailing silence. It was quite an intimidating setting, and in the all-pervading loneliness, it had all the ingredients to frighten us terribly.

Minutes felt like hours as our limbs, burdened by fatigue, sank into the benches, leading us to recline and try taking a nap. Yet, fear and loneliness prevented us from falling asleep. We were unable to figure out the next course of action. Both of us had been utterly drained of energy, and our eyelids involuntarily surrendered to exhaustion. Spending the entire night in that isolated place seemed like a daunting task, but we had no other options. While lying on the creaky wooden bench, I saw in the faint ambient light a nebulous figure coming down from the temple precincts. A chilling sensation ran through me, and I realized we were no longer alone there.

The mysterious figure, in a sketchy profile, slowly glided towards the lamppost right across the road and positioned itself beneath the banyan tree. As my eyes became accustomed to the faint light around the banyan tree and its surroundings, the features of the imposing figure became increasingly distinct to me. It was a tall, robust man, and his muscular physique was amply conspicuous in the tender shine of the streetlight. He stood still, his gaze fixed on us.

He continued to stand beneath the banyan tree, staring at us. While he held a hurricane lamp in his left hand, an axe gracefully rested on his right shoulder, and its gleaming metallic edge created tremendous anxiety in me. He was wearing a cord of twisted strands, embellished with 'rudraksha' beads, around his neck, while two smaller bands of similar beads were tied around his massive biceps, resembling bulging orbs. The lower part of his stout frame was clad in a simple loincloth, one end of which was elegantly tucked inside from behind. His forehead and upper arms were smeared with holy ash. The matted hair, parted in the middle, cascaded over his broad shoulders. A thick, whopping moustache gracefully twirled up above his upper lip, and a dense, long, flowing beard covered the chin area and extended downward.

Gently patting Suma awake, I rose from my bench to face the man standing a few yards in front. Suma held my hand firmly, standing behind me. The man walked slowly towards us with remarkable grace and poise, while we watched him advance with great caution and apprehension. He came very close and positioned himself within striking distance. While I knew I was no match for his superior physical standard, I did not want to put Suma in harm's way. In a gentle and heavenly voice, he sought to know why we were standing in that deserted place at such a late hour. His voice, despite its calmness, carried an air of authority. For me, it was intimidatory, and with great effort, I wanted to say something, camouflaging my nervousness, but words eluded me.

Quickly assessing my petrified state, he took a few steps closer, and keeping the hurricane lamp down, he placed his heavy left hand on my shoulder. I immediately noticed a change in his countenance; the tough look had given way to a warm and disarming smile. The sincerity in his smile and the twinkle in his eyes rapidly eased my anxieties, and my unease began to dissipate. He once again wanted to know why we were there all alone and cautioned that the location was not ideal for a young couple like us to be at such an unearthly hour. On hearing our story, he briefly lapsed into a pensive mood, and, showing an element of empathy, he offered to take us to a place where we could safely spend the night until the next morning. Given his amiable demeanour and the absence of other viable alternatives, we were tempted to place our trust in him and follow his lead, lest we be left to endure the night at the bus stop.

He walked ahead, raising the hurricane lamp a bit high to illuminate our path as we followed. We ambled along the embankments of paddy fields, then ventured through a patch of land filled with tall, swaying plants. A cool breeze whizzed through the wild and overgrown grass, creating an eerie atmosphere. The gentle moonlight and the light from the hurricane lamp cast unusual profiles on the ground, guiding us through the marshy terrain. The soft mud beneath our feet writhed and created strange sounds as we walked.

After walking for some time, we entered what appeared to be a dense forest, with towering canopies of overgrown trees nearly touching the sky. The air carried the scents of damp earth and wildflowers, making us feel that we were immersed in the heart of nature. As we ventured deeper, the thick overhead branches of trees obscured the moonlight completely, leaving the hurricane lamp as our sole source of illumination. The sounds of crickets and the occasional hooting of owls broke the domineering silence, creating a disconcerting atmosphere. Unperturbed by these sounds, the man continued to lead us without looking back even once.

Finally, our walk ended at an old, ramshackle house that looked like it hadn't been used in many years. He leaned his axe against a wall in a corner and gently pushed open the fragile-looking front door of the house. The metallic hinges of the door made a squeaking sound as they parted ways, showing us the way in. I took a moment to survey the surroundings. We were in the middle of a dreary landscape, where the ceaseless wind whispered disquieting tunes through gnarled trees. Amid the thick vegetation, the house looked very much out of place, creating an air of mystery and gloom. Time had not been kind to this abandoned dwelling. Moss and ivy had claimed parts of its decaying walls, giving the impression of skeletal hands reaching out for something long lost. Bats circled above the house, expressing their displeasure at the unwelcome intrusion by flying in all directions.

The man led us inside, and we climbed the cracked stone steps at the entrance, following him into the house. The place held a strange feeling for me as I observed it in total disarray. The windows had dirty, shattered glass, and cobwebs covered the corners of the walls, forming a complex network of delicate threads that underscored the fact that time had taken its toll on the interior.

Faint moonlight filtered through the shattered windowpanes, bringing in stray beams of light that partially illuminated the front room. In the bright glow emitted by the hurricane lamp, we could see a pile of antique, decaying furniture arranged haphazardly: chairs with damaged legs, an upturned table, and a cracked mirror reflecting distorted images of us, all evoking a feeling of dejection. The remnants of forgotten possessions hinted at past lives that had once thrived within these walls, now faded into the relentless passage of time.

The air was heavy with suspense, making every step inside the house feel like trespassing into a realm of spirits and phantoms. Sensing our confusion and melancholy, the man assured us not to worry about the condition of the room we had entered. He guided us into another room, and to our surprise, it looked spick-and-span. The room had an antique-looking wooden cot with crisp linens neatly draped over a thick mattress. He advised us to relax until the next morning and left the hurricane lamp in the room for us to use before swiftly disappearing into the thick darkness. Mysteriously, there was no trace of him along the pathway, as if the darkness had swallowed him up. Everything unfolded so rapidly that we couldn't even convey our gratitude to him for all the help he had rendered to us.

Suma and I exchanged glances that conveyed various emotions and feelings. We felt that the place, at least, seemed safe enough to spend the night. As there was no lock to secure the room from the inside, we dragged a broken sofa and placed it across the main door to ensure that no one entered the house while we slept. Reclining on the cot in the bedroom, I reflected on the events of the late evening and postulated that the mysterious man might have been a woodcutter returning home late, possessing a generous heart to aid a couple in distress by offering the use of what appeared to be a house he was familiar with. The night passed peacefully, with the gentle whispers of the breeze serenading the compound. Nothing disrupted our slumber, and we enjoyed a peaceful sleep.

We awoke to the cheerful chirping of birds and quickly ran through our morning routines. The bathroom, though a bit old, served its purpose well. The tap initially appeared dry and in disuse, but to our surprise, when we turned it on, water flowed with good force. With our morning tasks done, we planned to visit the temple once again before leaving the place. Although we couldn't express our gratitude to the man for his assistance, we felt it was a fitting gesture to thank the deity for the indirect favour granted to us when things looked dire the previous night.

In the daylight, the house appeared far more run-down than what it looked in the night. Complete silence surrounded us, and the nearby trees appeared to huddle together, as if they, too, were wary of drawing too close to the ominous house.

Walking through the densely vegetated area and then crossing the vast stretch of paddy fields, we arrived at the banyan tree. From there, we could get a clear view of the magnificent temple. At the temple, we met the same limping oracle, engaged in conversation with another middle-aged man and his wife near the pond.

Inside the temple, we met the priest, and after finishing our prayers, he handed us prasadam on a banana leaf. The raised eyebrows on his face, however, suggested that he had a few questions for us, which he did not want to ask within the sacred confines. After the darshan, when we came out, he quickly followed suit, closely tailing us.

Outside, the oracle was still in conversation with the middle-aged man and his wife, but as soon as he saw us emerging from the inner shrine, he rushed over. The priest and the husband-wife duo also joined him. All of them appeared surprised to find us there in the morning, looking refreshed after our morning bath. As far as they knew, there were no nearby places that could have provided us with overnight accommodation and allowed us to return to the temple for the morning darshan. They were all eager to know where we had spent the night and how we managed to make it to the temple for the morning darshan. I narrated the entire story of our night's adventure, leaving them amazed and dumfounded.

While the incident left everyone in a state of confusion regarding the identity of the Good Samaritan, who had appeared out of nowhere to assist us in our moment of distress, the priest recounted a similar story from his memory that had occurred in his early days as a priest. This incident also involved a young couple who had travelled from a distant place to visit the temple and became stranded. They, too, received help from a stranger in a similar manner, who carried an axe and was never seen in the area before or after.

The temple was once very popular in the olden days but had gradually fallen into a state of neglect. Concerned about the erosion of its fame over time, the temple administrators sought to find remedies through an extensive astrological examination. From their findings, the astrologers deduced that a palpable void permeated the sacred space, leaving it bereft of the divine energy that once imbued it with reverence and spirituality. They found that the aura of divinity had waned, transforming the temple into a mere architectural shell, devoid of the enchantment that once drew worshippers seeking solace and connection. Recognizing the urgent need for restoration, the astrologers recommended the comprehensive renovation of the entire structure, coupled with the daily performance of pooja.

One of the revelations that surfaced pertained to the origin of the temple. It was discovered that Lord Parshuram had erected the temple several centuries ago in reverence for Lord Shiva and his consort, Parvati. Based on the planetary positions, the astrological examination threw light on clear indications of Lord Parashuram's continued divine influence on the temple premises. The deteriorated state of the temple stirred his wrath, prompting him to periodically visit the premises at odd times to avoid the attention of the common man. He was aghast at the lackadaisical manner in which the sacred place was being run.

Soon, the administrators launched renovation efforts on a war footing. Once the work began, the local panchayath body also pitched in by initiating a bus service from Thaliparamba to a nearby village, passing by the temple, to make the place more accessible to devotees. Unfortunately, due to the unavailability of sufficient funds, most of the planned improvements remained on paper, and the project found itself in the doldrums.

As we were preparing to leave in order to catch the morning bus, the middle-aged couple offered us a ride to Thaliparamba in their car. I had noticed their car parked by the banyan tree. Gratefully accepting their offer, we bid farewell to the priest and the oracle before making our way to the car.

During the drive to Thaliparamba, the man gave a brief introduction to himself. He was the branch manager of a nationalized bank in Kannur, and, after retirement, he and his family chose to settle in a village near Thaliparamba. He had been a regular visitor to the temple in the past, though his visits had become less frequent due to health issues and other commitments.

We arrived in Thaliparamba, and after thanking him and his wife profusely, we hurried towards the ticket booking counter. While awaiting the train, I kept asking myself if the man who had appeared the previous night to assist us was really Lord Parashuram himself or merely a woodcutter heading home after a day's hectic work. I wasn't sure. Yet, according to the revelations from the astrological examination, it had to be Lord Parashuram, and it gave me goosebumps all over.

CHAPTER TWELVE

THE GHOST WHO CAME TO WATCH TELEVISION

Shriwardhan, a coastal village in the Raigad district of Maharashtra renowned for its pristine sandy beaches, gained infamy after a series of bomb blasts devastated the city of Mumbai in 1993, claiming the lives of over two hundred and fifty people. The RDX used to trigger these blasts was clandestinely landed in Shekhadi, a less frequented coast of Shriwardhan, and then transported to Mumbai via road, evading the vigilant eyes of various anti-smuggling agencies and the police.

The Marine & Preventive Wing of the Customs Department was the agency entrusted with the task of checking anti-smuggling activities along the coastal areas of the state. This incident caught the department unawares and dealt a severe blow to the agency's reputation. In order to tide over this serious lapse, the department devised comprehensive strategies to enhance surveillance in vulnerable coastal areas of Maharashtra, fortifying the ongoing efforts against smuggling. As part of this initiative, several batches of new officers were deployed to Shriwardhan to infuse new energy into the existing system.

My turn to join the teams in these operations at Shriwardhan came in 1998. Our batch consisted of ten officers, divided into three groups, each comprising three officers. Our group had four officers to avoid fractions, but this arrangement did not cause any friction with the other groups. Fortunately for us, this turned out to be advantageous should any unexpected situation arise for any member of our group. Due to the considerable distance between Shriwardhan and Mumbai, it wasn't feasible for the officers stationed in Shriwardhan to make daily commutes from their homes.

There was an acute problem with accommodation on rent in Shriwardhan. The officers from the previous batch had been residing in the office rooms. The office was situated in a three-bedroom apartment, but our batch was quite particular about not residing there. So, immediately after joining, all of us collectively agreed on renting a house, and Patil, our driver, who was very influential in the area, assisted us in finding one quite easily.

The house was a bit far from the office and situated in an isolated spot overlooking the Shriwardhan-Alibaug road. A narrow, muddy, yet motorable road led from the main road to our house. Since we were privileged to use our departmental jeep, commuting to the office and back didn't pose much of a problem. The area around the house was exceptionally quiet, with no other houses nearby. This calm atmosphere was the perfect recipe for us to unwind and enjoy a good sleep after the long grind of patrolling.

The slow-paced life in Shriwardhan was a big irritant for me, especially after having been accustomed to the fast-paced Mumbai lifestyle for nearly two decades Nevertheless, life had to move forward, and I gradually assimilated myself into the local way of life. Since there were no stores or markets in close proximity, Patil took charge of procuring all the essentials required for our week-long survival. Our responsibilities primarily involved conducting anti-smuggling operations, which encompassed both sea and road patrolling during the day and night. After a strenuous week of hectic activities, we returned home, looking forward to a well-deserved two-week break.

On one occasion, a member of our group, Vivek, was unable to join us in Shriwardhan due to indisposition. As a result, the remaining three of us had to assume his responsibilities. I willingly took on the responsibility of morning sea patrolling and night road patrolling, while my colleagues, Ashok and Abhay, managed the two shifts of night sea patrolling.

Coincidentally, during this period, our jeep was out of action as it had been sent for periodic servicing, rendering it unavailable for night patrols for the entire week. This unexpected turn of events proved to be a stroke of luck for me, providing relief from night road patrolling and allowing me a good night's sleep at home.

As usual, Ashok and Abhay left for their night patrol at 7 in the evening. I finished my dinner by 8 p.m. and then spent a couple of hours watching TV before retiring to bed around 10 p.m. Usually, once I hit the bed, I wouldn't wake up until 6 in the morning. However, on that night, I awoke in the middle of the night, needing a bathroom break. While returning to my bedroom, I noticed that the TV was on, playing some music in the living room. Wondering if I had forgotten to switch it off before going to sleep, I picked up the remote and turned off the TV before heading back to my bedroom.

The next day, the same thing happened. I was awakened in the middle of the night by the blaring sound of the TV in the living room. Since I distinctly remembered switching off the TV set before going to bed, I assumed that either Ashok or Abhay might have returned home after calling off their patrolling early. Without bothering to check who it was, I went back to sleep after closing my bedroom door.

The next morning, seeing both Ashok and Abhay return home together gave me a mild shock. I had the impression that one of them might still be sleeping in their bedroom after returning early from patrolling and watching TV late into the night. If it wasn't either of them, then who could have been the one watching TV late at night? This thought troubled me throughout the day, as I was pretty sure I had switched off the contraption before going to sleep.

Since I had turned it off using the remote control, I suspected that it had some glitch causing it to turn the TV on by itself. I chose not to air my concerns to Ashok and Abhay because I knew they might assume I had been in high spirits the night before and forgot to switch off the TV.

Once again, on the third night, the same thing happened. The TV blared at a high volume, waking me up once more, and I was awfully irked. The previous night, I had switched off the TV at the power source, making it clear that the problem was not with the remote, as I had initially assumed. Fuming in anger, I dashed to the living room and switched it off again at the plug point. As I was about to return, I caught a glimpse of a hazy figure sitting on the sofa. Initially, I thought it might be the shadow of something fluttering outside in the mild breeze and didn't pay much attention. However, as I was about to exit the room, I heard the tinkling sound of bangles. It banished my sleep and brought me to my senses. I stopped there and turned the light on.

A woman, veiled in a flowing white saree that seemed to undulate like mist, sat cross-legged at one end of the sofa. Her long, black hair dropped down her shoulders, its dark tendrils brushing against the breeze from outside. Her pallid face, with large, bright eyes burning like fiery balls even in the bright fluorescent light of the room, sent shivers down my spine. She gave me a witheringly imperious look, perhaps angered by the interruption in her TV-watching session.

My legs appeared rooted to the ground as panic reigned all over me, leaving my mouth parched. Somehow, I managed to dart back to my bedroom, hastily shutting the door behind me. Gasping for breath, I knelt on the floor, my knees succumbing to an involuntary tremor. The sensation was akin to an unseen force, causing them to shatter and jerk uncontrollably. I braced for her imminent intrusion into the room, and the mere thought curdled my blood. The ordeal was harrowing, with my heart pounding like a diesel generator set. After a few agonizing minutes, the sound of the television died down, and soon after, I heard the sounds of receding footsteps fading into the night.

Until dawn, I lay on my bed, unable to sleep. As the first rays of the sun streamed through the windows, I rose. After ensuring that everything was normal, I cautiously stepped out of the bedroom. A couple of hours later, Ashok and Abhay returned home. Realizing the importance of allowing them much-needed rest during the day, I refrained from divulging the incident to them, as I was averse to creating unnecessary panic in their minds. Shortly after, Patil, came to pick me up for the office on his motorbike.

While patrolling, I took one of my trusted sepoys, Gharat, to the side of the boat and recounted the spine-chilling incident. To my surprise, he appeared least perturbed. With a cryptic smile playing on his face, Gharat disclosed that most of his fellow sepoys were well aware of the haunted history of that house. However, they chose to keep this information under wraps, fearing the wrath of Patil, the driver. The Patils held a formidable disposition and considerable sway within Shriwardhan and its neighbouring areas.

Expecting a repeat of the unsettling incidents in the ensuing night as well, I joined Ashok and Abhay on their night patrol. Concealing my true intention by framing it as an opportunity to share some light-hearted moments on board the vessel, I spent the night alternating between Ashok's and Abhay's boats. Since our duty schedule for the week was concluding in two days' time, it was not a tough ask for me to continue to be on board the boats on all shifts.

Two days later, the shift of our batch concluded, and we set off on our journey back home for a well-earned two-week hibernation. During the drive back to Mumbai, I casually mentioned to Ashok and Abhay about my tryst with a ghostly spirit that would come to watch TV in the house at night. They were dumbstruck. Recovering from the shock, Ashok revealed that he too had noticed some unexplainable things happenings in the house during the daytime when he rested after night patrols. He had seen the ceiling fan working in the living room several time, even after switching it off. He had dismissed it off assuming that it was due to a malfunction of the switch. This spurred Abhay also to divulge some strange things that he had witnessed in the bathroom. The taps turned on after he came out of the bathroom turning them off. Perhaps they believed that continuous night duties had disrupted their biological clocks, attributing the stray incidents to these disruptions. As a result, these incidents remained tucked away in the recesses of their minds, never surfacing openly. The drive back home provided the first opportunity of the week for all of us to be together once again.

A week into our cooling-off period, I received a call from Ashok. He said that one day, our fellow officer Ramamurthy also had a face-off with the same ghostly lady who used to appear in our house at night to watch TV. This news created a flutter among the other officers, who held an emergency meeting the following morning, determined to find an alternative residence immediately. Fortunately, within two days, they managed to find one much closer to the office and shifted to the new house on the same day. During the intervening period, Ramamurthy emulated what I did during my time and spent the nights on the boat with his colleague, who was on night patrol.

A week later, we resumed our duty in Shriwardhan. The officers of the batch we had relieved assured us that the new house was free from the presence of any mysterious spirits, and no one intruded at night to watch TV shows. Driver, Patil, while on road patrol tried to playdown the ghost story, terming it as the ingenious creation of Ramamurthy, who found the previous house not to his liking and far from the office Little did he know that he was trying to reason with someone who had the rare honour of sharing the roof with a ghost, watching TV in the living room while he slept in the bedroom.

CHAPTER THIRTEEN

BRUSH WITH DANGER: SLITHERY SCARE IN THE NIGHT

After two years of enduring the demanding lifestyle in Shriwardhan, the relentless wheel of time spun once more, and I found myself relocated to the Mora Customs office. Mora, an endearing coastal town situated near the port of Uran, was in stark contrast to the faraway and unforgiving Shriwardhan. Essentially a one-horse town, Mora boasted a placid atmosphere with a populace as warm and welcoming as the coastal city's primaeval shoreline.

The shift to Mora brought about a welcome change, affording me to spend a lot more time at home. It was the proximity of Mora to my residence that allowed me to return in the mornings after completing night shifts. This convenience marked a striking departure from the isolation and distance that had defined life in Shriwardhan.

Situated facing the port, the Mora Customs office offered a breathtaking and idyllic view of the vast expanse of the Arabian Sea, creating a splendid backdrop of boundless beauty. The cool sea breeze, carrying the briny scent of the ocean, became a source of energy and cheerfulness for me. In contrast to the inexorable sea patrolling in the rough waters of Shriwardhan, Mora offered a far more relaxed duty structure. There was only one session of sea patrol, which took place during the night. Each night, we would randomly cruise around the areas of the Gateway of India, Butcher Island, and Elephanta Island on a boat hired by the department from a private operator. The boat reminded me of an antique piece normally found in museums. Meanwhile, the departmental jeep used for road patrols was as old as the Customs Act and, more often than not, needed to be goaded into action. It was vulnerable to mood swings, and its roadworthiness was always suspect.

After finishing the night sea patrols around midnight, I would retire to sleep in the office room. Returning home past midnight was not a feasible option, and I was forced to sleep in the office room, much to my displeasure. The room, which would put even a dungeon to shame, was far from ideal for spending the night after tiresome patrolling. A flickering bulb hung from a frayed wire at its centre, struggling hard to illuminate the interiors. Gaping openings in the ceiling revealed the night sky and scattered stars, offering an unusual form of stargazing within the confines of this dreary space. In the corners of the room, cobwebs formed intricate patterns on the crumbling plaster of the damp walls. The room bore a perpetual fusty smell. A pigeonhole window let in just a bit of light and a lot more dusty air, making the room even more malodorous and unpleasant. The rickety cot looked like it might fall apart at any moment. A dusty, old ceiling fan, hanging on a rusty pole, wobbled as it tried to circulate the stuffy air to all parts, and the creaking sound it made while revolving on the corroded beam made sleep difficult.

Outside, the on-duty driver and two sepoys slept on benches on the veranda. With the break of dawn, the duty driver would drop me off at home, and this routine went on smoothly. Patrolling in the cool and refreshing sea breeze on board the boat at night always served as a precursor to blissful sleep.

It was no different on that day as well. Returning from patrol, I settled on the rickety cot, gracefully surrendering to a comforting sleep in the whirring lullaby provided by the ceiling fan above. As I began to drift off to sleep, something landed on my chest with a thud, abruptly jolting me awake. In reflex, I flung off the sheet that covered me and quickly sat up in bed. Although I was sure that the heavy object had fallen from the ceiling, I could not see it in the dimly lit room. However, the sudden hissing sounds coming from beneath the cot confirmed what it was, and fear washed over me. Springing out of bed hastily, I switched on the light. In the flickering light, I spotted two cobras slithering into view from under the cot, with their hoods raised and bodies entangled. They were engaged in a fierce battle. Deftly moving away from them, I rushed outside and woke up our driver.

The driver alerted the two sepoys who were sleeping nearby. Armed with sticks, they cautiously entered the room. In that moment, fond memories of the sacred place in the compound of our house back in Kerala, dedicated to snake worship, flashed in my mind. During our childhood, our parents instilled in us the practice of revering snakes and emphasized the importance of coexisting harmoniously with these creatures in the vast universe. They advised us never to harm any reptiles unless absolutely necessary. So, I made it explicitly clear to the sepoys not to harm the snakes. It was a battle of attrition between them, and I had no business interfering in it. One of the reptiles was in very bad shape, and if the fight continued, it would certainly succumb to its injuries. Not wanting that to happen inside my room, I instructed the sepoys to carefully guide them out into the wilds across the road.

With great care and skill, the sepoys managed to steer the two venomous intruders out of the room without causing them harm. As the cobras slithered away into the thick bushes, I felt a huge sense of relief at the unexpected event I had just gone through.

Suddenly, it struck me that those reptiles had crash-landed from the ceiling onto my chest, and there was every possibility that either of them had bitten me, whether by mistake or intention, immediately upon their fall. I became extremely nervous, and sensing my concern, the driver closely inspected my torso with his flashlight. Fortunately, there were no bite marks on my body. The cobras, deeply engrossed in their fierce battle, had not considered biting the person who unwittingly provided them with a safe landing spot.

After that incident, I refrained from sleeping in the office room after night boat patrols. It was nothing short of providence that two deadly poisonous reptiles, engaged in a fierce clash, seemingly oblivious to their natural instincts, forgot to dip their lethal fangs into the person on whom they landed. Perhaps it was the cumulative effects of the worship we had been performing back home to keep the serpents in good humour that saved me the day.

CHAPTER FOURTEEN

CHILLS IN THE NIGHT: A GHOST IN THE TOILET

It was the late nineties, and one of my close friends, Sanjeeb Chakraborty, was on duty at the Customs office in Chiplun. He was due for repatriation to his parent department, the Central Excise, in about a week. Sanjeeb used to lavishly extol the historical richness and beauty of Chiplun, urging me to visit the place before his transfer from there. Although I had passed through Chiplun several times while traveling to Kerala by train on the Konkan Railway route, I never had the opportunity to explore the town. So, this was going to be my last chance to take advantage of the occasion and allow my dear friend Sanjeeb to be the perfect host for me for a couple of days in Chiplun. I did not want to let it slip away.

Boarding the Mangala Lakshadweep Express early in the morning from Panvel, I reached Chiplun around 11 a.m. Sanjeeb had assured me that he would be at the station to pick me up in his departmental jeep. However, there was no trace of Sanjeeb on the platform. Presuming he would be waiting for me outside the station concourse, I walked towards the exit lobby.

Sanjeeb was not there either. Knowing well that he had a reputation for being a late riser, I didn't rule out the possibility of him arriving late at the station. Chiplun was famous for its vada pav, and many passengers would purchase this popular snack while passing through the area. Since Sanjeeb had not yet arrived, I decided to enjoy a bite of vada pav while waiting in a corner, away from the hustle and bustle of the lobby at the exit point. As I sank my teeth into the piping hot vada pav, the sight of a jeep racing towards the station, kicking up lots of dust, grabbed my attention, and I was certain it was Sanjeeb. Indeed, it was him. With a sheepish smile on his face, he warmly greeted me and offered profuse apologies for the delay, attributing it to the poor road conditions en route. We then headed to his quarters in the jeep.

The journey to his place took around a half-hour drive, navigating through craggy and uneven roads marked with pits and broken patches. Along the way, Sanjeeb asked the driver to halt the jeep at a wayside hotel so that we could enjoy a hearty breakfast. The vada pav at the station was not good enough to fully satisfy the raging hunger in my belly. The driver soon found a good hotel, run by a husband and wife, and stopped the jeep in front of it. There, we had poha, a popular and delicious Maharashtrian breakfast, which effectively alleviated the hunger pangs that had been raising their ugly heads again and again. A piping-hot cup of tea washed down the poha before we resumed our journey.

The jeep sped past a lengthy stretch of paddy fields, and soon we entered a lush, green area. Remarkably remote, it was surrounded by thick vegetation on one side and a barren hillock on the other, with a river meandering in between. After about ten more minutes, we arrived at an old building snuggled in a secluded landscape, and the driver brought the jeep to a stop. With a twinkle in his eyes, Sanjeeb told me that this was his guesthouse. He then pointed to another small standalone structure a few hundred metres away, indicating that it was his office.

Unlocking the front door, Sanjeeb led me inside. The house consisted of a single bedroom, a small drawing room, and a kitchen, but it was good enough for one or two people to stay comfortably. The only drawback was the absence of a bathroom inside. Sanjeeb took his baths outdoors by drawing water from the kitchen well. He showed me a small thatched shed a few meters away, and with a mischievous smile, he said it was the toilet. A closer look revealed that the door of the so-called toilet was crafted by joining two broken asbestos sheets together. While the vast blue sky above served as its roof, the clouds during the day and the stars at night acted as silent guardians over the activities that took place within its squalid enclosure.

Sanjeeb dismissed the services of the jeep and asked the driver to report back after lunch. The house was in a beautiful setting, surrounded by lush greenery on all sides. Tired after the four-hour train journey, I longed to take an open-air bath by drawing water from the well. The well water was very cold, thanks to the December weather, and the bath left me feeling quite refreshed. After changing into formal attire, I joined Sanjeeb in the drawing room for a chat. Meeting after a long time, we spent an hour catching up on everything that had happened in between.

Around 1 PM, a middle-aged woman arrived with a tiffin carrier, handed it to Sanjeeb, and quickly departed. She was the wife of his office driver, and Sanjeeb's regular meals came from their home. The sight of the four large containers in the carrier brought a smile to my face, and without any further delay, we sat down to have our lunch.

A few minutes after we finished our lunch, the driver arrived with the jeep, and we set forth on our expedition to explore the interiors of Chiplun village and countryside. Doubling as our guide, the driver went on to brief us on the history and geography of Chiplun along the way. Situated on the banks of the Vashishti River, Chiplun had several notable places to visit, including the Vashishti River, Marleshwar Temple, Guhagar Beach, Parashuram Temple, and Sawatsada Waterfalls. He first took us to the 155-year-old library in Chiplun called Lokmanya Tilak Smarak Vachan Mandir, which housed a large collection of rare books and ancient artefacts.

While returning from there, he drove us around the white-sand beaches and beautiful mango and cashew groves by the Vashishti

River. We then headed towards the Parashuram Temple, located 10 km from Chiplun. The temple was one of the few temples dedicated to the 6th avatar of Vishnu, known as Parashurama. The temple consisted of a central shrine surrounded by two smaller buildings. In the main temple, there was an idol of Parashurama in the centre, flanked by the idols of Brahma and Shiva on the left and right, respectively. The architecture of the temple reflected influences from Hindu, Muslim, and European styles.

By the time we reached Guhagar Beach, it was late evening. The sparsely populated beach offered a serene ambiance, and we spent an hour relaxing on its white sands. A handful of tender coconut vendors were doing brisk business on the beach, and the sight of them generated a good amount of thirst in me. Towing Sanjeeb with me, I approached one of them, and together we enjoyed a couple of cool, refreshing tender coconuts, relishing the taste of their sweet water against the backdrop of the mesmerizing sunset. As darkness descended, we decided to head back.

At the guesthouse, our dinner had already arrived, and the sight of the tiffin carrier resting near the doorway was a pleasing sight to me. The day had been so hectic and grinding that we badly wanted to go to sleep after a quick dinner. Also, there wasn't anything better to do in that isolated house After dinner, I chose to sleep on the sofa in the drawing room since the bedroom had only a small cot. The sofa seemed to be a much better option than sleeping on the floor with a mat.

It was the dead of night when I woke up, compelled by the relentless call of nature. The copious amount of tender coconut water at the beach in the evening was taking its toll on my bladder, making it impossible to ignore any longer.

In my groggy state, I opened the main door and, putting on a pair of sandals I found outside, headed towards the toilet. In the subtle glow of the waning moon, I walked up to the thatched shed a few meters away. With a soft kick of my foot, I nudged the door open. Just as I was about to enter, my heart stopped beating at the terrifying sight inside.

A woman in a white saree was standing in a dark corner of the toilet, with her back to me. The creaking sound of the door made her turn her head towards me with a disconcerting motion. Strangely, her head rotated a full 180 degrees on her neck without moving the body. Her eyes seemed to dangle from their sockets, as if they were brutally gouged out. A malicious expression contorted her face. Her drooping eyes locked with mine in a hideous stare, freezing me in place. The scene was horrifying, and I felt as if I might drop dead right there. With all my might, I sprinted back, shrieking loudly all the way.

In sheer terror, I ran back to the guesthouse as fast as I could. Waking Sanjeeb up from his bedroom, I recounted the frightening sight I had just witnessed in the thatched toilet shed. Though not fully convinced, he accompanied me to check out the place. The toilet door was ajar. Sanjeeb, flicking on an electrical switch hanging outside on a small iron pole, cautiously peered inside. In the dim light, he found no one inside. Turning back, Sanjeeb mockingly suggested that it was just something my drowsy mind had conjured. However, my mind kept insisting that it was not so, and there was definitely someone inside when I opened the door. Gathering courage, I moved closer, looking over Sanjeeb's shoulder. There was no one inside.

As we made our way back, an unexpected sight brought us to a sudden standstill. There, on the half wall of the well near the kitchen, sat the same woman. Her long hair hung loose, and she was casually running her fingers through the cascading locks. I was numb with fright, and my feet, as if rooted to the earth, refused to respond to my instinctive urge to flee. Sanjeeb, standing next to me, turned pale and visibly frightened. As we fumbled to gather our wits, the woman slowly rose from there, swiveling her neck around, throwing a terrifying stare at us, and then freewheeled her way into the darkness, gradually disappearing from our sight.

Hurrying back to the house, we secured all the doors and gathered anxiously in the bedroom. In the early hours, the idea of slipping into a snooze until morning seemed too far-fetched. It took a while for my pounding heart to return to its regular rhythm and function normally. Sanjeeb, still looking pale, seemed to be reflecting on the fact that he had been living in the guesthouse with a mysterious woman visitor all these days. It wasn't surprising, considering that he hadn't ventured into the guesthouse's toilet even once during his stay, as he had told me the day before. For minor needs, he preferred the open air, while for more complex tasks, he relied on his office toilet, which was cleaner and offered more privacy.

The pleasant sight of sunlight streaks appeared on the horizon, bringing us a feeling of hope and safety. Sanjeeb had made up his mind to vacate the guesthouse and had packed all his belongings while remaining awake overnight. It was a wretched place, and he did not want to stay there a minute longer. I also quickly stuffed all my things back into my backpack and was ready to move out. Meanwhile, Sanjeeb called his driver and asked him to bring the jeep as early as possible. On our way back, he briefed the driver about all that had happened during the night.

At the office, the driver arranged for a cup of tea for us. While we were having tea, a young boy arrived there. He was Swapnil, one of Sanjeeb's staff members, who might have been called in early by the driver.

After finishing our tea, Sanjeeb briefed Swapnil on the situation, and he listened very attentively. I was surprised by Swapnil's expression and reaction; it seemed as if this was nothing new to him, as if he was accustomed to hearing about such occurrences in the house. Without saying a word, he invited us to his home for breakfast. His house was conveniently located near the office, allowing us to freshen up and enjoy a much-needed bath to rejuvenate ourselves.

At his house, Swapnil's mother graciously served us a delicious khichdi made of sago for breakfast, which was just what I needed at that moment. While we sipped our tea, Swapnil spoke about a tale that circulated among the local community about the ghastly murder of a woman that had taken place in that house many years ago. Many people propagated stories of having seen a ghostly figure near the toilet during the night. The house originally belonged to a Maharashtrian family, but they didn't stay there for long; in fact, they left just a few days after moving in. Despite their best efforts to sell the property, they couldn't find any takers. No one was willing to buy a haunted house.

During that period, he continued, the Customs Department was actively seeking a residence to serve as a guesthouse for its staff, and that's when they discovered this particular house. The haunted reputation attached to the property didn't dissuade any of the officers involved, given the pressing need for accommodation for officers arriving from Mumbai and other distant locations on postings in Chiplun. Capitalizing on the opportunity, the department efficiently finalized the lease agreement at a significantly reduced rate, much to the delight of the higher-ups. The inauguration was marked with grandeur, featuring a local MLA. However, due to the deteriorated condition of the house, owing to a lack of proper maintenance, none of the officers posted there chose to stay in the house. Instead, they opted to use the office premises for their accommodation needs.

The question that popped up in my mind was why the haunted nature of the house wasn't disclosed to Sanjeeb before he moved in. Swapnil had an explanation for that as well. Sanjeeb strongly disliked using the office for accommodation due to his peculiar habit of sleeping late into the morning hours, a practice he had religiously adhered to for as long as he could remember. He was concerned that the cleaning staff, who reported for duty very early in the morning, would disrupt the well-established routine of his lifestyle. As a habitual late riser who had rarely witnessed a sunrise in his adult life, he might have believed that residing in the office could impose an unwanted element of structure and discipline in his immutable life—something he was eager to avoid.

Now, the major concern that seemed to bother Sanjeeb was finding a roof to stay under in Chiplun for the next few days. He clearly did not wish to return to that foreboding house, and staying in the office was also not a viable option due to the harsh realities prevailing there. His repatriation to his parent office had already been confirmed, and he was waiting to receive the relieving message by wireless in a couple of days.

As Sanjeeb slipped into a pensive mood, Swapnil offered a suggestion. He told Sanjeeb that he could stay at his house until the order relieving him was received from the headquarters.

After a while, the driver arrived with the jeep, and we decided to quickly complete our sightseeing of the remaining places since I had a train to catch later in the afternoon bound for Panvel.

After a whirlwind tour of all the remaining places on our original schedule, Sanjeeb dropped me off at Chiplun station. The Kochuveli Bhavnagar T Express train was fairly occupied, but I managed to find a vacant lower berth. Bidding adieu to Chiplun, I settled down on it to enjoy the five-hour-long journey.

When the train reached Roha, the cacophony of tea vendors' cries outside brought me to my senses. The thought of a hot cup of tea was too tempting to resist, and as I moved towards the front-side exit, I noticed a woman in a white sari seated a few rows ahead of mine. When I passed her, our eyes met, and she gave me a radiant smile, which made me very uncomfortable since a woman in white had caused considerable turmoil for me the previous night. Without acknowledging her smile, I continued ahead to get my cup of tea.

While sipping the hot tea, I speculated whether this was the same woman who had made a mess of our last night, still hot on my trail. After finishing my tea, I boarded the train from the rear door, wanting to avoid another confrontation with her.

An hour later, the train reached Panvel, and I cautiously moved towards the exit door, deliberately avoiding a glance at the seat the woman in white sari had occupied. As I approached the exit, I found her standing at the doorway, ready to disembark. Maintaining some distance, I stood a few paces behind her. Sensing my presence, she turned around and gave me a smile. To my immense relief, her head didn't swivel around the neck; instead, she turned her body to look at me. As she did, I noticed a nameplate pinned to her sari. It made me realize that ghosts don't typically travel on trains, especially not with a nameplate on their costumes. It was then that I finally caught my breath, assuming that she was a nurse from a hospital heading home after completing her shift.

CHAPTER FIFTEEN

SOUL THAT CAME TO QUENCH ITS THIRST

While posted at the Mumbai International Airport, I frequently undertook official trips to Calicut, averaging about three visits per month. The choice of destination was at times optional, and owing to its proximity to my hometown, I used to prefer Calicut since it held a special significance for me compared to other destinations. During those days, my mother was grappling with a plethora of frailties, leading to a gradual deterioration in the condition of her health. Consequently, I wished to spend as much time as possible with her in the twilight zone of her life.

At the destinations, it was the responsibility of Indian Airlines to arrange suitable accommodation for the visiting officers. In Calicut, the airlines had designated two excellent hotels for this purpose. Usually, I chose not to stay in those hotels and instead went straight home which was around 65 kilometres from the airport. The airlines arranged a car, and the driver, Suresh Babu, was the one who regularly drove me down. A home visit afforded me a stay of four days with my mother.

However, on one occasion, the regular routine went for a toss due to a flash strike in Calicut caused by unfortunate violence between two political party groups. Chaos ensued throughout the city, disrupting the entire transportation system. Suresh Babu briefed me on the situation and cautioned that, due to the sudden strike, it was fraught with risk to go home, let alone reach the designated hotel in the city. Taking cognizance of the prevailing situation, the airlines had arranged a homestay accommodation very close to the airport for my overnight stay.

Suresh Babu collected the keys to the house from the airline's duty officer, and we began our drive to the location. During the journey, he informed me that the house was newly constructed and situated on a hillside in Karippur. The owner had originally intended to reside there, simultaneously using it as a homestay for guests. However, due to a lukewarm response, he moved to another house in Calicut. The house was located in a remote area away from the city, and perhaps it did not attract the attention of tourists or travelers as he thought it would. While there was a caretaker to maintain and keep the house spruced up all the time, he rarely visited the place. The absence of shops in the vicinity was another hurdle for obtaining essential food items. Suresh Babu tried to cheer me up by reassuring me that it was just a matter of one day and I could get through it without much trouble.

To address the immediate problem of food for my dinner and breakfast, Suresh Babu suggested that I buy essential items from a shop along our route. Finding a decent-looking hotel on the outskirts of Calicut, he stopped the car in front of it, and we placed an order for a parcel of chicken biriyani. The hotel had partially closed its shutters, indicating that they were all set to shut down the shop, apprehending potential trouble and violence from the protesting people. While the workers hurriedly prepared the biriyani, they offered us a cup of tea to pass the time. Within ten minutes, the biriyani arrived, neatly packed in an attractive plastic container. From the adjacent provision store, I bought two bottles of Bisleri, a loaf of bread, and half a dozen plantains. Equipped with these supplies, we continued on our way to the house. In approximately fifteen minutes, we reached our destination, and

Suresh Babu left, assuring me that he would return an hour before my flight back to Mumbai the next morning.

The house bore a spooky look, standing alone in the dark. The disorderly and contorted trees, growing wildly and extending over the area like a canopy, created an awfully freakish appearance around the house. The absence of proper caretaking was glaringly evident and reflected poorly in its compound. The sit-out had loads of dust scattered all over, but unmindful of it, I entered the house. Climbing the creaky wooden stairs, I proceeded to the bedroom upstairs, where a faint musty smell greeted me. Placing the loaf of bread and bananas on a nearby table and the bottles of water on the broad windowsill, I pushed the windows open to let the cold winter breeze sweep in. The hinges registered their protest with a gentle yet jarring noise as they opened reluctantly. The fresh air brought some relief to the stuffy smell that filled the room. The sight of a small mosque across the road and a massive graveyard beside it brought memories of an old movie into my mind. Layers of mist outside draped a magical veil over the area. The setting sun painted the mist in golden hues, casting long shadows over countless tombstones in the graveyard.

After a refreshing wash and a change of clothes, I settled onto the cozy bed with a couple of pillows supporting my back. With nothing else to do in the room and being alone, I felt inclined to have an early dinner. The sight of the biriyani in the container was tempting, especially since the meagre in-flight meal had failed to satisfy the hunger gnawing in my belly. Eagerly, I opened the parcel of biriyani and emptied its contents, relishing every morsel with the crisp air from outside, enhancing the dining experience.

The entire area outside was in absolute darkness due to the absence of streetlights, and the faint moonlight tried valiantly to lighten the surroundings as best as it could. The suffusive darkness and deafening silence impelled me to retire early. Switching off the lights, I slipped under the bedsheet, hoping for a peaceful sleep in the night.

However, the silence proved to be transient and was shattered by the sound of a water bottle tumbling down to the floor. It jolted me awake, and groping for the switch in the darkness for a while, I finally managed to switch on the lights. In the bright light, I found one of the water bottles missing from the window sill and lying on the floor. Assuming it had been pushed down by the mischievous wind, I picked it up and placed it on the nearby table before going back to bed once again.

As I began to drift back to sleep once again, another sound interrupted my blissful sleep. By then, the room was reasonably lit up by the moonlight's luminosity, and without needing to switch on the lights, I discovered that it was now the other bottle's turn to take a tumble. However, I was horrified to witness a ghastly sight—a partially decomposed hand, its flesh clinging in patches to exposed bones, furtively withdrawing from the window grills into the shadows outside. The finger bones and the raw bones on the lower and upper arm of a skeletal hand presented a truly disconcerting sight. Standing stupefied in the darkness for a while, I watched the hand reappear and fumble, as if desperately searching for something. Soon, it withdrew itself once again and disappeared from sight.

Mustering courage, I scurried towards the window to secure it properly, only to find that the locking hook was in a tampered condition. As I struggled desperately to fix it, something clutched at my lungi, tugging at it with force. Shockingly, it was the same skeletal hand that had reappeared from the other side of the window. I frantically attempted to fend off the rotting hand, and in the tussle, my hands accidentally made contact with its cold, putrefied flesh, soaked in blood, creating a repulsive sensation in me. Eventually, I had to part with my lungi to liberate myself from the grip of the abominable hand. Having failed in its attempt, the hand once again withdrew itself before disappearing into the darkness outside. It was a horrific struggle that lasted a good couple of minutes.

The grapple resulted in a few bloody scratch marks on my thigh, leaving a reminder of the agonizing struggle. It was difficult to sleep after the ordeal, and I took a deep breath to try to calm my jangled nerves. Apprehensive of any possible repeat of the hand's intrusion through the window, I spent the night sitting on the bed, staring into the darkness. Fortunately, nothing happened again that night.

The break of dawn unveiled the horizon with a gentle crescendo of light, bringing a lot of relief to me, but the horrid effects of that harrowing night were not easy to shake off. Suresh Babu arrived in the morning to pick me up. I did not speak a word about the incident to him and sat through the half-hour drive in silence.

Back in Mumbai, I confided in one of my close relatives known for his keen insights into paranormal theories about the incident. The interpretation he provided had a peculiar angle to it, yet it appeared credible to some extent. According to him, the hand, even in its partially decomposed state, was desperately seeking water to satisfy the soul's craving—a basic necessity denied in the final moments of departing from one's body. Evidently, the soul had departed its body without anyone offering a few drops of water in those final moments. However, what puzzled me was why only the hand appeared to be seeking water and not the entire body. He had an answer for that as well, explaining that all other body parts would have decomposed completely by then, leaving only the hand with some flesh and bones, enabling it to pursue its quest for the elusive water.

The shocking narrative suggested a poignant conclusion: the mysterious hand sought a few drops of water, not with malice but with a desperate yearning to quench the thirst of the wandering soul. Perhaps the hand was a tool of the soul in this pursuit. This explained why, in many cultures, water was offered to a person on the cusp of death to gratify the departing soul. In Hinduism, it was Ganga Jal, while other religions had their own holy waters serving this purpose.

But in this instance, the skeletal hand chose my Bisleri water to quench the soul's thirst. Unfortunately, due to its frail nature or infirmity, the hand lacked the strength in its bones and flesh to execute the task. It tried twice, failing on both occasions and dropping the bottles. It would have been a great tagline for the company's advertisement campaign if the hand had been successful in its attempts: 'Bisleri: The Choice of Spirits and Mortals Alike.'

CHAPTER SIXTEEN

INHERITED VENDETTA: A TALE OF RETRIBUTION

After completing my assignments at Shriwardhan and Mora Port, I was transferred to the Belapur circle for the remainder of my tenure in the Customs Preventive department. Belapur was in close proximity to my home, providing a more relaxed lifestyle. Moreover, the absence of a coastline within its jurisdiction meant relief from gruelling sea patrols. Apart from dealing with the monotony of attending numerous court cases and conducting road patrols at night, the Belapur posting did not entail a significant amount of work.

The days passed smoothly, and after almost a year, it was time for me to be repatriated to my parent department of Central Excise. Finally, the order was issued in August, right in the midst of the peak Ganesh festival celebrations in Mumbai. However, the repatriation order was kept on hold temporarily due to the ongoing Ganesh festival. The festival of Ganesh Chaturthi was one of the most celebrated festivals among Hindus, symbolizing the auspicious occasion of Lord Ganesha's birth. Mumbai, in particular, vibrated with a frenzied devotion as it eagerly welcomed the annual homecoming of Lord Ganesh. Across the city, both households and pandals were decked up with idols of Lord Ganesh. The fervour and grandeur exhibited by the people during that festival created a great amount of religious devotion within the hearts of the faithful.

The Belapur circle office was no exception to the festivities that captured the entire region of Mumbai and the state of Maharashtra. The spirit of celebration had rubbed off on the entire staff, and the office was bedecked with flower decorations and various types of festoons all over the building. Since most of the Maharashtrian officers were on leave due to the Ganesh festival, I had to perform road patrolling on every night during those ten days. However, the sepoys and the driver did not have any exemption from attending their duty.

On the previous day of Ganpati immersion, the office sported a deserted look, with almost everyone staying off from duty, leaving me with no one to accompany for the night road patrolling. It was certain that I would be relieved of my duties in a day or two, and I did not want to skip the duty in the dying moments of my tenure in the Belapur Customs Circle.

Just as I was about to get into the office jeep, Mukund Pawar, one of our drivers, happened to drop in at the office for some work. Observing that I was all alone, he expressed his willingness to accompany me on the patrol. Since he was on leave, I didn't want him to sacrifice his holiday, so I suggested that he return home and participate in the festivities there. Mukund had a Ganpati idol installed at home, scheduled for immersion the following day. However, he seemed determined to join me for reasons I did not know, and both of us set out for patrolling.

As Mukund started the ignition, he requested that we make a visit to his house on the way for a darshan of his Ganpati idol and have dinner there. While I was fine with the brief stopover to pay deference to the Ganpati at his home, the invitation for dinner did not entice me since I had already had a full meal before starting for the office.

Mukund's house was a small tenement decorated with shimmering, tiny electric bulbs that sparkled and illuminated the magnificent Ganpati idol placed on an exquisitely erected miniature pandal made of thermocol. The moment I stepped inside, all the family members greeted me with familial love and respect, a culture synonymous with the Maharashtrian community. Mukund proudly introduced me to his mother, wife, and his little five-year-old son, who was busy distributing prasadam to all the devotees dropping in to offer their prayers. After I offered my prayers to Lord Ganpati, Mukund's wife served me a generous portion of prasadam, an assortment of treats rich in ghee and sugar with a sprinkling of raisins and cashews that stimulated my taste buds in a delightful way.

As it was time for me to leave for patrolling, I once again offered Mukund the option to stay back and enjoy this auspicious time with his loved ones. However, he was not willing to leave me alone for patrolling.

As we drove through the outskirts of our jurisdiction in the dead of night, Mukund opened up, describing the challenges he had faced on the family front. Poverty, property disputes, the death of his father, and various other hardships marked the early years of his life, disrupting his academic pursuits and compelling him to discontinue education after completing SSC. Three hours passed quickly, and as we approached the narrow and congested road leading to the magnificent Kararja fort, Mukund expressed a desire to stop the jeep and spend a few minutes there. The allure of the moonlit surroundings and the calm atmosphere enchanted me. Mukund parked the jeep on one side of the road, and we disembarked. The road was completely deserted, with no signs of any houses anywhere nearby. We sat on a large rock, likely displaced from the adjacent Karanja hills and wedged at the base of towering trees along the roadside.

We sat there quietly for a few minutes, enjoying the hushed silence. Breaking the deafening quietude, Mukund picked up where he had left off. I felt compassion for his past struggles and didn't want to deter him from sharing his experiences with me if it would lessen his feelings. Perhaps he intended to tell me something more complex, given the serious tone he had started with. Also, he was aware that I was soon to be relieved from the Belapur circle office in a day or two, and this might be our last patrol together, as another driver would be on duty the next day.

Mukund pointed out a sharp turn a few meters ahead on the side where we were sitting, and in a choked voice, told me that it was where his father had died in a gruesome road accident. I had already heard about his father's death since it had been a topic of discussion among the sepoys in the office. As we both gazed into the darkness, he continued in a raspy voice, revealing that it wasn't an accident but a brutal murder carried out in cold blood. I was shocked to hear this revelation and stared at his face. Without shifting his gaze, Mukund told me that on that fateful day, his father was returning from the market when his bike was struck by a jeep coming from the opposite direction. The impact of the collision was so severe that it threw him off his bike several meters away, where his head struck a large boulder at the roadside. Tragically, a few days later, he succumbed to his injuries in the hospital. This untimely death had devastated Mukund, and he fell into depression, which took him months to recover from.

Even in the pitch-black darkness, I could see his eyes glistening with tears, and his voice grew hoarse. I sat quietly, attempting to gauge the depth of sorrow Mukund was enduring. He then disclosed to me something extremely mystifying that had happened on the day his father died in the hospital. His father had been in a coma for several days, and the doctors had ruled out any chance of revival due to the severe head injury sustained in the accident. However, just a few minutes before losing the battle, he opened his eyes, tightly held Mukund's hands, and muttered something to him. His last words both appalled and enraged Mukund beyond measure.

In his last words, Mukund's father conveyed to him that his departure from this world was only ephemeral and he would return sooner than later, as he had an unfinished task to accomplish – to deliver just retribution to someone for a crime committed. With those words, he closed his eyes and took his final breath.

Mukund carried this thought always with him, carefully guarding it from being revealed to anyone, even in his immediate family. Mukund's life took an extraordinary turn when he became a father himself and was blessed with a baby boy, Vijay. As Vijay grew up, he exhibited certain peculiar traits. Even as a toddler, his behaviour bore a striking resemblance to Mukund's deceased father, and when he began to speak, he astonished the family by recalling memories of a previous life. He eloquently related details of his past existence, disclosing names and even incidents that had occurred long before his birth. To everyone's amazement, he identified almost everyone in their family album, even those he had not met, seen, or heard of. A particular photo of a man named Sadanand Mhatre with Mukund's father caught Vijay's attention. Sadanand Mhatre had once been a close friend of Mukund's father but later fell out due to a boundary dispute. This dispute remained unresolved despite the involvement of the village sarpanch, other respected individuals, and senior politicians from the village.

The abrupt change in Vijay's expression upon seeing the photograph of Sadanand Mhatre surprised Mukund. There was no way his son could have seen or heard about Sadanand, as their relationships were irreparably strained. Also, Mukund never used to discuss the property dispute in front of his parents or his son because he believed it was a battle he was destined to lose. Thus, it always remained an elephant in the room for the family. Sadanand Mhatre, the man who had usurped their land, was an influential figure in the village, and no one had the gumption to stand up or speak against him.

The oddities in Vijay's early behavioural patterns were brushed off as a minor aberration by his family. They considered the possibility of it being a case of split personality, hoping that as he grew older, he would become a normal human being.

Days passed, and one day Mukund took Vijay for a bike ride to Karanja Fort. When they reached the narrow, sharp turn on the road leading to the fort, Vijay asked his father to stop the bike and get down. Standing there for a few minutes, he seemed to be experiencing a sense of déjà vu. Suddenly, his expression became very unusual, a wave of emotions flashing over him. For a moment, Mukund felt like he was seeing his father in Vijay because his face momentarily bore the characteristics of his father's. Settling quietly down under a tree, Vijay told Mukund that this was the exact spot where the jeep had collided with the bike he was riding. He pointed to a large stone on the left side, where he had struck his head after being knocked down. Mukund was stunned, as he had never disclosed the exact place where the accident had taken place. Vijay went on to describe the horrifying incident in detail, as if he were the one hit by the jeep and killed.

As Mukund paused, taking a moment to heave a deep sigh, memories of several similar stories I had read in newspapers flashed through my mind. I thought this might be another account along the same lines. However, what Mukund then told me was so unbelievable that I found myself staring at his blank face in disbelief. He revealed that Vijay was well aware of every detail of the bike accident and claimed that it was a staged incident. According to Vijay, he was the re-embodiment of his grandfather and insisted that he was the one who had lost his life in that very accident—a revelation that Mukund struggled to believe. Nevertheless, he had to believe his son because, as Vijay recapped the story, his facial expressions and voice bore an extraordinary resemblance to those of his father. This left Mukund with the strange sensation that his father was communicating with him through his son, Vijay.

After a momentary pause, Mukund resumed. According to Vijay, while he was riding his bike back from the market, a jeep coming from the opposite direction collided with him at a sharp curve on the Mora Karanja Road. The impact was so devastating that it sent him flying off his bike, crashing into a grove, and striking his head against a rock. He remained conscious briefly and clearly saw the person at the wheel of the jeep—it was Sadanand Mhatre.

Sadanand slowly dismounted from the jeep and approached him. Bleeding profusely, he pleaded with Sadanand to take him to a hospital. However, Sadanand ruthlessly turned his back on him and casually walked away. As he got into his jeep and drove off quickly, he made an appalling declaration that it was all part of a sinister plan to eliminate him to secure control over the disputed piece of land entangled in the border issue.

After recovering from my shock, I enquired Mukund why the police hadn't conducted a thorough investigation into the matter and incriminated Sadanand Mhatre on charges of murder. He replied that while the police had registered a murder case against an unknown person, their investigations never dared reach the killer due to the enormous clout he wielded. Mukund suspected that the police possessed enough evidence to book him but stopped short of taking any action due to his social standing and wealthy disposition in the area. The case file gathered dust in their records, and Mukund's attempts to revive it were met with staunch resistance.

However, Mukund possessed clinching evidence provided by the 'deceased' himself, but he was unable to raise even a finger against the person he intended to confront. His opponent was mighty and ruthlessly resourceful, so Mukund bided his time, awaiting the right opportunity to seek vengeance.

Following Mukund's father's demise, Sadanand Mhatre seized control of the disputed property and erected a permanent boundary wall, blatantly disregarding all laws and regulations. With no one willing to challenge him or speak out against this violation of rights, the property gradually became one of his many uncontested possessions.

It was 3 in the morning, time for us to leave, but Mukund wasn't finished. The last words of his father, spoken at the time of his death, seemed to echo in his thoughts day and night. Clenching his fist, he expressed his determination to seek retribution for a heinous crime committed against his father. However, he remained doubtful about his ability to assume the role of an executioner and carry out the sentence pronounced by his father on his deathbed.

Vijay, whom Mukund believed to be the reincarnation of his father, consistently motivated and reminded him of their impending mission. However, their plan of action faced many obstacles, leading them to abort in despair and helplessness at the crucial moment. Perhaps fear for the law and the future of his family restrained him from taking the extreme step of seeking vengeance on Sadanand Mhatre.

One late night, while Mukund was asleep, he woke up to see a hazy image of his father sitting by the side of his bed, smiling, as if trying to jog his memory about the unfinished task. Similar incidents of sightings continued to happen frequently, adding to the immense pressure he was already under. The weight of not fulfilling his father's death wish had become unbearable for him. Rising from his seat, Mukund came very close to me. In a voice as cold and chilling as the icy Himalayan winds, he revealed that he had hatched a plan. It froze me completely.

After a moment of silence, Mukund confided that he had already conducted a few dry runs in recent days to identify Sadanand Mhatre's exact residence and daily routine. From his findings, he discovered that Sadanand Mhatre went for a morning walk along the same Mora Karanja Road every day. I sensed the implication of his words, and it weighed heavily on my heart. I also understood the depth of his grief and his overwhelming desire to seek retribution, whether it meant taking the life of Sadanand Mhatre or spending his remaining life behind bars in peace and contentment. He did not appear to care about his family or his budding son.

My attempts to mollify him by advising about the perils of taking the law into one's own hands, especially for someone in government service, did not produce the desired results. Stressing the importance of seeking justice through proper channels, I requested that he refrain from taking any rash actions that could lead to disaster and risk causing more harm than good. Assuring him of my unstinted support in finding lawful ways to hold the culprit accountable for his actions, I told him that together we could explore legal avenues to reveal the truth and ensure that justice prevailed.

I stressed the importance of approaching the police once more, urging them to reopen the case and conduct a thorough reinvestigation. He said he had already taken this step a few months ago, but the police rejected his request outright. Attempting to dissuade him from the potentially perilous path he was considering, I apprised him of a few stories of others who, like him, had ventured down the path of revenge, only to be consumed by misery and remorse. I was aware that his emotions had clouded his judgement, making my attempts at reasoning futile. It was time for us to leave, and as a final push, I held his hands and tried to drive home the message that Vijay, purportedly the reincarnation of his father, might be a result of an extraordinary phenomenon. His words, therefore, should not be seen as the definitive determinants of the future for him and his family.

The first rays of dawn began to break on the horizon, and I hoped the arrival of a new day would bring about a change in the mindset of Mukund, possibly deterring him from pursuing justice through unlawful means. He dropped me off at my home and then proceeded to the office to park the jeep. That was the last I saw of him for many days.

Two days later, I was relieved from the Belapur Customs Circle office to join my new posting in the Central Excise office in the CGO Complex in Belapur. About a week later, during a tea break in the canteen, I noticed a group of sepoys engaged in conversation at the adjacent table with a Marathi newspaper in front of them. Since most of them were known to me, I asked one of them what was so exciting in the news that they were reading and discussing widely. He brought the newspaper over and showed me a report that carried news about the death of a prominent citizen from Karanja village in a hit-and-run motorcycle accident.

My heart fluttered as my worst fears came true – the man killed was none other than Sadanand Mhatre. It was a hit and run murder. Carefully scanning the report, I discovered that, fortunately, there were no eyewitnesses to the accident, leaving the police clueless.

Finishing my tea quickly, I left the canteen, even as the sepoys waxed eloquent about the stature of the deceased. On reaching the lobby, I noticed the staff leaving the office in droves, causing a chaotic situation in front of the elevators. Soon, I realized that it was the result of a spontaneous call for a bandh issued by a few political outfits in response to the murder of Sadanand Mhatre.

It was a Friday, and two days later I received a call from Mukund saying that he was standing at the security gate of my housing society and requested that I come down for a minute. I quickly went down and found Mukund standing outside near his motorbike, beaming with happiness. Smiling at me, he said in Marathi that he had accomplished the task and was feeling at peace now. The ghost-like figure, which used to stalk him at home and sit by his bedside, appeared on the same night Sadanand Mhatre was killed. It blessed him, raising both hands, seemingly pleased with the turn of events. When I asked if his son was aware of the developments, he threw a contended smile at me and pointed towards the back seat of his bike. In a whisper, he told me that while he executed the death wish of his father, his son Vijay watched the incident, riding pillion on the bike.

In those brief five minutes of conversation, he continually expressed his relief and happiness over the incident. To him, both his father in the heavens and the one reborn in this world would be gratified to witness the fulfilment of the entrusted task. He held my hands briefly before turning to mount his motorbike, which had been a witness to the gory incident that occurred four days ago. As he rode away, a mix of emotions churned within me. I felt a terrible sadness for Mukund, yet the overriding feeling was one of unalloyed happiness, seeing that he had put the issue behind him and appeared very much at peace with himself now. The glimmer of contentment in his eyes was a testimony to the overwhelming relief that he experienced after fulfilling what he believed was a sacred purpose. I sincerely hoped that the police would not succeed in cracking the case for lack of evidence, offsetting their failure to nab the culprit in the cold-blooded murder of Mukund's father.

CHAPTER SEVENTEEN

SINISTER HAUNTS: A VENGEFUL HIGHWAY SPECTRE

Retirement marked a turning point for Suma and me. After working tirelessly for over 35 years in our respective fields, we felt the need for a quieter life away from the crowded city of Mumbai to unwind and plan our immediate future ahead. It set us on a course of thought that eventually led us to make a groundbreaking decision: to relocate ourselves to the cultural capital of Kerala—Thrissur. However, after two years of intermittent stays there, the initial charm of the new location died down, and we began to yearn for the vibrant city of Mumbai. Nothing stood in the way of our resolve to wrap things up and return to Mumbai, immersing ourselves once again in the familiar rhythm of life. To add a touch of excitement and make the return journey more memorable, with a touch of adventure, we opted to drive back to Mumbai in our car.

After painstakingly studying various route options, we carefully planned our trip, choosing the scenic route via National Highway 48. The route we charted would take us through several beautiful places, including Palakkad, Coimbatore, Salem, Bangalore, Hubli, Belgaum, Kolhapur, and Pune, before reaching our final destination in Mumbai.

On the scheduled day of leaving Thrissur, we hit the road just as the morning skyline painted the sky with vibrant hues, and the sun gently appeared on the horizon. The continuous soundtrack of devotional songs provided a soothing melody in the background as the car sped towards Palakkad. As we drove, we witnessed the beautiful sight of small houses with delicate plumes of smoke gracefully rising from their thatched roofs—a telltale sign of bustling kitchen activities within. The lush green paddy fields added a touch of rustic charm to the surrounding scenery. Passing through the incredible Kuthiran tunnel was a breathtaking experience. As we entered this well-illuminated, cavernous expanse, it became an experience in itself.

Leaving Palakkad behind, we headed towards Coimbatore, eagerly looking forward to a well-deserved breakfast. At exactly 7:30, we arrived in Coimbatore and took a half-hour break to refuel ourselves.

Resuming our drive at 8 o'clock, we covered the distance to Salem in just two and a half hours, making a brief pit stop at a petrol pump to fill petrol. Our intention was to reach Bangalore for a late lunch, and we maintained a decent speed, with the speedometer consistently hovering around the one-hundred mark, ensuring a swift and comfortable journey along the beautiful highway.

By 1:30 in the afternoon, we arrived in Bangalore. A clean-looking vegetarian hotel on the wayside beckoned us for lunch. Our next stop was Hubli, where we planned to spend the night. It was a 6-hour drive from Bangalore, indicating that we needed to start no later than 2 in the afternoon in order to reach there by 7:30 or 8.00 p.m.

Back behind the wheel, we kicked off our journey around 2 in the afternoon. It was a bit hectic, as driving immediately after a meal posed a challenge, but I was game for it. The drive from Bangalore to Hubli along the vast, dry landscapes was not a pleasant experience. The continuous songs playing from the car's music system provided a comforting background, allowing Suma to steal a brief nap. As I had a target to meet, I remained focused on my task and maintained a fair speed all through.

By 7:30 p.m. we reached the city of Hubli. The city looked charming and attractive, with bustling streets alive with the warm, inviting gleam of streetlights and the vibrant colours of neon signs from shops and businesses. The boy at a nearby petrol pump, where we had stopped for refueling, had suggested 'The Fern Residency' for a comfortable stay. Using the assistance of Google Maps, we located the hotel easily. It was a nice-looking hotel, more than adequate to rejuvenate us and prepare us for the next day's drive to Belgaum and beyond.

The morning greeted us with the first rays of the rising sun unveiling the beauty of Hubli. The city, set against the backdrop of the stunning Western Ghats was graced with dazzling lakes and beautiful green landscapes, captivating us with its charm. Since our next stop, Belgaum, was just a short two-hour drive from Hubli, we made a slight adjustment to the plans and delayed our departure until the afternoon. Moreover, our scheduled overnight stop was at Kolhapur, which was another two-and-a-half-hour drive from Belgaum, so we felt our planned itinerary was right on course, confident enough to reach there before nightfall.

After enjoying a hearty breakfast, we explored the city of Hubli in a hired cab, returning in time for lunch. Following our meal and a half-hour nap to reinvigorate ourselves, we hit the road again, leaving Hubli at 2 in the afternoon, well-rested and much refreshed.

Around 4 in the afternoon, we reached Belgaum and stopped to take a tea break at a roadside restaurant. By 4:30, we were back on the road, heading towards Kolhapur—the final leg of our journey for the day. Our aim was to arrive in Kolhapur by 7 in the evening, so we enjoyed a leisurely drive, relishing the scenic beauty along the route.

Driving through the picturesque countryside was a true delight, with the sun radiating a warm shine over the lush fields and winding roads. As we traversed numerous villages in the vast Belgaum district, the sun began to dip behind the horizon, gradually giving way to darkness. Just after we crossed a village called Halatti, the car's headlights began to play some mischief, flickering continuously. By the time we reached a small village named Vidya Nagar, they conked out completely, throwing us into a spot of bother.

Without headlights, driving in the darkness became risky, as the streetlights spaced far apart along the road did not offer sufficient light. I pulled the car over to the side of the road and got out, utterly dejected, facing the growing darkness all around. I attempted to flag down some passing cars for help, but unfortunately, no one stopped to check on us or offer assistance.

With a fretful heart, I checked our surroundings desperately for any sign of help. Suddenly my eyes met the sticker of Kia Roadside Assistance neatly pasted on the front windscreen of the car. In an instant, I took out my phone and dialed their number. A voice answered, politely asking for my credentials. He inquired about the problem with the car and our exact location. The man assured me that help would reach us as quickly as possible. Relieved to hear that, I got back into the car. Since the car was running low on fuel and we had another hour-long drive to reach Kolhapur, I turned the ignition off. Lowering the car's front side window shutters halfway to invite fresh air, we remained inside patiently, awaiting the arrival of the Kia Roadside Assistance team. The gentle evening breeze provided a calming effect, tempting me fall into a snooze, but my posture was not conducive to that. Adjusting the backrest a few notches lower, I languidly settled into my driving seat with my eyes closed, while Suma occupied herself by browsing the internet on her mobile phone.

A gentle whiff of a potent floral fragrance wafted through the air, tickling my senses as I dozed. I presumed it came from the nearby wilderness. However, my musings were abruptly interrupted by a soft knock on my half-open window. I opened my eyes to check if the Kia service team had arrived, but instead, I was met with the pixelated face of a mysterious woman, dressed in pleasing attire, visible through the fog-ridden glass of the window pane. Lowering the glass further down, I observed that her head was veiled with a red scarf, covering most of her face. She appeared unusually polite, regarding me with a courteous smile. In a husky voice, she attempted to say something that I couldn't comprehend. Noticing my discomfiture with the language, she repeated her words, supplementing them with gestures and actions. From her expressions, I construed that she was asking why we had ended up stranded on the roadside in such a remote and deserted location. Realizing that Marathi was widely spoken in the region between Belgaum and Kolhapur, I tried to explain to her in that language the reason why we were there and told her that help was on its way. With gestures continuing to substitute words, she invited us to her home to spend the time until the mechanics arrived, expressing concern that the location was not safe for a couple like us.

Given my inherent nature to trust people and take them at face value, I found nothing wrong with her suggestion. It was also not certain how much more time the mechanics would take to arrive, and I had no desire to remain cramped inside the car until then. Moreover, I was badly in need of a cup of tea to feel refreshed before resuming the hour-long drive to Kolhapur. On the other hand, Suma appeared circumspect about the idea, concerned about the potential risks associated with accepting an invitation from an unfamiliar woman offering to take us to her house in an unfamiliar place about which we had little knowledge.

In the end, her indecipherable words, accompanied by her actions, had their way. Throwing Suma's sceptical glances and caution to the wind, I made up my mind to follow the stranger woman to her house. With Suma in tow, we followed her into a narrow, dark alley, discreetly maintaining a safe distance and leaving a few paces between us. The safe zone afforded me some space to calm Suma's ruffled feathers. While she walked effortlessly in the darkness, giving us the impression that she was very familiar with the path, we relied on the flashlights on our mobile phones to follow her. The dense vegetation flanking both sides hindered the moonlight from making the alley clearly visible in the darkness.

There were no houses on either side, and as we proceeded along the alley, the narrow path seemed to stretch endlessly. Even after a few minutes of walking, the woman in front showed no sign of stopping, and I became a little bit edgy. A few yards ahead, I noticed a makeshift gate made of bamboo sticks, leading to a thatched house. When she reached the gate, I called out to her, wanting to ask how much more time it would take to reach her house. She paused and, gently turning back, removed her scarf, revealing the contours of her full face. Her appearance was horrifying, with droplets of blood dripping from her dreadful visage. Her eyes, scorching and emitting fire, her disheveled hair floating wildly in the wind, and a tattered sari fluttering around her spectral form left us frozen in our tracks. Then, she let out haunting laughter that pierced the silence of the place. As she advanced menacingly with her eyes fixed on us, I clutched Suma's hand in a flash, yelling at her to run quickly onto the main road.

In the grip of absolute fright, we sprinted through the narrow, dark alley, our hearts pounding vigorously. Twice, my feet tripped over the knotty roots of trees that crisscrossed the ground along the alley. Each time, I quickly regained my footing, and together we continued until we finally reached the safety of the main road.

Finally, when we reached the main road, I noticed another white Kia car parked right behind ours, bringing a lot of relief as we knew the roadside assistance had arrived. I approached them, introduced myself, and one of the team members instructed me to follow them in our car for a short distance ahead. We proceeded without headlights for nearly half a kilometer before halting the car when the RSA team pulled over ahead. The place was brightly lit under the signboard of a Canara Bank branch, providing ample light for them to examine our car.

Observing our scruffy appearance and my soiled clothing, they were curious to know if anything had happened to us while waiting for the RSA team. As they opened the car's bonnet and inspected the systems, I briefed them about the harrowing incident, fully aware that it would be hard for anyone to believe. However, to my surprise, one of the two men belonged to a village near Vidhya Nagar and had heard stories of similar occurrences in the past.

As the man worked on the car's electrical system under the bonnet, he recounted stories of similar incidents that had befallen other travellers in the same location. Many years ago, a young woman tragically lost her life in a hit-and-run incident near Vidhya Nagar. Struck by a speeding car, she was flung into a nearby thicket, and her badly mangled body was only discovered a couple of days later when locals detected a foul smell emanating from the underbrush. She had suffered multiple injuries and died of severe bleeding. Afterwards, many travelers claimed to have seen the ghost of the woman jaywalking along the roads at night. The Kia RSA team frequently received distress calls from that particular location during late evenings. Locals widely believed that her spirit lurked in the area, perhaps seeking to find the car that hit her. They also believed that the woman's spirit possessed a remarkable ability to interfere with the electronic systems of cars, causing them to go haywire and leaving travellers stranded.

The Kia team resolved the headlight issue in ten minutes, and we resumed our journey to Kolhapur shortly after. However, the unnerving encounter with the ghostly woman in Vidhya Nagar left us with niggling disquiet. I observed Suma occasionally throwing worried glances at the rearview mirror, perhaps to confirm that the spectral figure of the woman was not trailing us. To dispel the spine-tingling feeling, we needed something cathartic, and I felt there was nothing better than a burst of loud music in the cabin. The spurt of music gradually dissipated the tension, and we drove forward confidently, basking in the brilliance of the street lamps.

Following our arrival in Kolhapur, we checked into Hotel Devgiri, situated at Uma Talkies Chowk. A rejuvenating shower washed away the day's fatigue, and a delightful dinner that followed further lifted our spirits. The next morning, we visited the renowned Mahalaxmi Temple in Kolhapur, an iconic place of worship in Maharashtra. After a hearty lunch, we began our journey back to Navi Mumbai, finally arriving home by late evening.